Vengeance

ALSO BY ZACHARY LAZAR

I Pity the Poor Immigrant
Evening's Empire: The Story of My Father's Murder
Sway
Aaron, Approximately

Vengeance

A Novel

Zachary Lazar

Catapult New York

First Catapult printing: February 2018

Photographs are by Deborah Luster, from her series *Tooth for an Eye: A Chorography of Violence in Orleans Parish*, and are used with her permission.

ISBN: 978-1-936787-77-7

Catapult titles are distributed to the trade by Publishers Group West
Phone: 866-400-5351

Library of Congress Control Number: 2017938491

Printed in the United States of America

10 9 8 7 6 5 4 3 2 1

For Deborah Luster

Ignorance about those who have disappeared
undermines the reality of the world.

—ZBIGNIEW HERBERT,
"Mr. Cogito on the Need for Precision"

I have often stared into the mirror and considered
the difference between the following statements:
    1) He looks guilty.
    2) He seems guilty.
    3) He appears guilty.
    4) He is guilty.

—PERCIVAL EVERETT,
Erasure

PART ONE

GLIMPSE

1

My friend Deborah, the photographer, once told me that she distrusts color, because it's too seductive—it prevents us from seeing what's really there. She wasn't speaking metaphorically, she was just explaining why she prefers to shoot in black and white, but in a larger sense she was talking about the rigor of looking, not glancing, not turning away. That first night we spent at Angola, we went outside to view the main prison under lights, the rectilinear massiveness of it, the fences and razor wire. I wanted to walk toward it across the vast lawn but Deborah said no, she'd heard there were snakes, so instead we walked down the road and made out two other camps in the distance across empty fields under the moonlight. I knew Angola was huge, but this was the first real sense I'd had of it. It was its own planet. That night, from the empty space around the Bachelor Officers' Quarters where we were to sleep, it was like when you're on an airplane coming into a foreign city in the dark and you see the different grid patterns of lights and gradually make out the vast shape of what's below. It was as if all the importance in the world had co-alesced in those fields—violence, punishment, collision, consequence—all that significance beyond the limits of my small understanding.

We got into Deborah's truck the next morning and followed the assistant warden, Cathy, from the BOQ past the main prison, then across the fields where a work gang was marching slowly in the glare and mist, carrying hoes straight upright against their shoulders, the angled blades a jagged clutter above their bowed heads. The workers were mostly black men, in cuffed jeans and pale blue shirts or white T-shirts, overseen by white men on horseback with guns. There was something pornographic about the scene, as if it had arisen out of someone's half-understood fanta-sies. The fields beyond spread out lush and green, the end-less landscape from last night now exposed in daylight. Angola had once been several adjacent slave plantations in central Louisiana. The original slaves were said to have been brought from Angola.

We had come to witness the rehearsal and produc-tion of a passion play, *The Life of Jesus Christ*, performed by Angola's inmates and their female counterparts from the nearby women's penitentiary in St. Gabriel. I write fiction, nonfiction, sometimes a hybrid of both, and I've tried to understand the impulse behind this blending—to under-stand that there's something I'm not seeing that most other people are (and I hope something I'm seeing that they're not). What I seem to resist is the idea that the real and the imaginary don't bleed into each other. Perhaps this is because what really happens in the world so often belies any notion of "realism." It was an implausible coincidence, for example, that had led Deborah and me to this project at Angola. Both of us had a parent who was murdered. Both murders happened in the same city, Phoenix, Arizona. They were both contract killings. I don't know how you'd calculate the odds of Deborah and I ever meeting after such an implausible coincidence, but many years later, after establishing our separate lives, we did meet, when I moved to New Orleans, where it turned out our houses were two blocks away from each other. You can see my roof from Deborah's roof. A strange coincidence—transformative, unbidden, like a fire. It seemed possible to me that by collaborating on this prison project, we might force this coincidence to become more than just an unlikely wound that we shared. As I wrote rather grandiloquently in my letter to the assistant warden, asking for permission to visit, I thought that by interpreting this play about the possibility of redemption in the wake of violence, Deborah and I might somehow enact "a kind of redemption of our own." That word, *redemption*, strikes me as dubious now, a sign not exactly of bad faith but of something inside myself I don't trust. That first night in the BOQ, I'd spread a thin sheet over one of the single beds in the dorm room and tried to read in that place usually occupied by guards sleeping between their shifts. The mattress was covered in plastic—even the pillow was covered in thick plastic. I examined my shoes and jeans and socks on the floor in the greenish, clinical light, and I felt within my dread of that place an uncomfortable wish to be there, that place where I didn't wish to be. Deborah had been there many times, photographing the inmates. They were ambiguous portraits, often beautiful and ugly at the same time. Of course shooting photographs in black and white is not an analogy for "seeing the world in black and white." On the contrary, the entire interest of black-and-white photography is in the infinite range of grays.

We parked outside the arena, the facility where they hold the prison rodeo twice each year, and I began to help Deborah with some of her equipment, but I could soon tell that she didn't want my help. Something about stepping outside the truck into the brightness and dust made us fretful, overly alert. It scrambled our signals, and somewhere in here I lost track of what was happening. I saw a camel standing in the dead grass outside the arena's gates— blond, tall, attended by two men in cowboy clothes, who looked at me without humor. Inside the arena, beyond the brown-painted gates and fences, men in work boots and jeans were still building the stage sets. So far, three wooden crosses bedecked with ropes had been raised on a mound of dirt. Beyond them, amid a few ranks of potted bushes and shrubs and a fake Roman temple made of plywood, a crowd of about seventy inmates was standing around chatting, the men in street clothes, the women from St. Gabriel in jeans and light blue shirts bearing the initials of the Louisiana Correctional Institute for Women in black letters. Cathy, the assistant warden, was responding to a call on her cell phone. Deborah had disappeared beneath the grandstand where she would set up for her photographs, formal portraits of the actors before a black velvet screen. The person who was supposed to be my escort had already lost interest and retreated far into the shade, texting. There were several animals involved in the production—the camel I'd just seen, some horses that now came charging across the arena at full speed—but the donkey, Cathy was learning now, had been quarantined because he had a communicable disease, and so maybe there would be no donkey this week. A woman who spoke with a Scottish accent was asking a prison employee what kinds of fruit they might find with which to bedeck the table for the Last Supper scene— were there melons, she asked, looking for something large enough for spectators to see from a distance—but no, there were no melons. Grapes? No—no grapes. Apples and oranges, that was pretty much it—apples and oranges, plus some bread. It was dawning on me, as I stood there watching all this, that the men working on the still-emerging sets with tape measures, levels, hammers, and saws were not hired carpenters but inmates. The man standing next to me in the Texas Longhorns cap with the Nikon camera was an inmate. He was a reporter for the prison magazine, he told me, covering the same story I was covering. A man who happens to be the son of God is betrayed, convicted, and sentenced to death. On the third day, he rises from the grave to save the world with a message not of retribution but of mercy.

As I said, I'd begun to lose track of what was happening

almost as soon as Deborah parked her truck, and this sensa-
tion didn't stop—I was alone, and began to wander, talking
to more and more people on the edges of the action, writing
down what they said, although little of it registered clearly.
When I wrote down the word *murder*, for example, it didn't
register much more than if I were a nurse writing the word
allergy in a medical chart. The reporter in the baseball cap
was a murderer. He'd set his girlfriend's house on fire then
shot her to death. I couldn't get this past act to match up
with his present—in the arena, he was just a middle-aged
man, small, soft-spoken, with a slightly sunken-in, sun-
burned face. Like almost every other inmate at Angola, he
was expected to die on the prison grounds. In Louisiana, a
life sentence literally means life. There's almost no parole.
The state also has the highest rate of incarceration of any
place in the world.

"A life sentence comes with an exclamation mark and
a question mark," one inmate told me. "Wow!" And then,
"When this gonna end?"

"Imagine you're trapped in a barn," another inmate said.
"Now imagine that the barn is on fire. You will do anything
you can to get out of that barn. You will do anything you
have to to get out of that barn."

Murder, kidnapping, rape, drug addiction, poverty,
abuse, all pointing to the terminus: life in prison. Deborah
had told me to come without expectations, to not prepare,
and it was true, I didn't need to prepare, or even ask any
questions beyond the most basic ones, but I didn't know
what a burden of information was there waiting for me. I

interviewed more than forty people over the course of that week, and what they told me filled up more than ninety pages of typewritten notes. After a while, I became an ear and an eye, nothing else. I found it impossible to go to the bathroom or even find a drink of water much of the time, because on my way to do either I would be interrupted with another story, another tragedy, another life presented for my appraisal.

Imagine you're trapped in a barn. Now imagine that the barn is on fire.

The inmate who said that was Kendrick King, who was thirty-one, in the ninth year of his life sentence. As it happened, I recognized his face from one of Deborah's photos—even in black and white, you could sense what Deborah called Kendrick's "Weimaraner eyes," a striking glint that in real life turned out to be the product of his caramel-colored irises. He was tall and wore knee-high rubber boots and a baseball cap with its bill folded in a way that made his face look gaunt, slightly spectral. He cuffed his jeans in meticulous folds over the tops of his boots. Because Deborah had mentioned him, and because I'd seen his photo, I'd looked up his case before we met, and that was how I knew that Kendrick King might be serving life for a murder he'd had nothing to do with. I still don't know if he had anything to do with it. When I tell friends this story, they look at me as if I'm naïve. What I tell them is that almost none of the inmates I spoke to that week claimed to be innocent. Even Kendrick King didn't make that claim until I prompted him by telling him what I knew. What I knew was what I read from the *Times-Picayune* of May 2, 2004:

A Jefferson Parish jury convicted a Westwego man for his role in a murder last year despite his claims that police coerced a confession from him.

Kendrick King, 22, will spend the rest of his life in prison, the mandatory sentence for second degree murder.

That first time we spoke, we stood in the shade and he told me his crime (murder) and his sentence (life without parole) and his roles in the play (Man in Crowd, Shepherd Three)—answers to the questions I asked everyone, which usually led to them telling me their whole life stories. As we talked, it came out that Kendrick's mother was from Saint Lucia and that he'd spent a part of his childhood in Crown Heights, Brooklyn, and so we made small talk for a while— the carnival parade in Crown Heights, the beef patties and the colorful flags of the different islands, the soca music and the reggae, those big vines of grapelike fruit whose thick skin you peel back to reveal the delicately flavored plumlike innards. Guineps. Ackee. We talked for a while like this, Kendrick bemused that I'd heard of any of these things, and then we compared cities—he'd lived in New York, Chicago, Houston, Dallas, Castries, New Orleans. I'd been to all of those places, including Castries, St. Lucia, so we traded some memories.

"I have to tell you," I finally said. "I know a little bit about your case. I mean, what was in the newspaper."

He looked at me, then examined his fingernails, his hand down by his waist.

"I guess what I'm trying to ask you is, it sounds like maybe you were pressured by the police to tell them about something you didn't do," I said.

"I didn't say anything. I never confessed to anything."

He stood with one of his feet against the wall, a hand braced on his bent knee, as if about to elaborate, but he seemed blocked by a sense of futility. Perhaps he'd told the story so many times that it no longer had a beginning or an end, only a series of entry points, and so there was no obvious place to start. The phone records that showed he was at his girlfriend's house at the time of the crime. The Mazda that his girlfriend had with her at work all day. The pair of shoes at his mother's house. I've since come to learn all the minutiae of Kendrick's case. When I try to explain it, I feel blocked myself—blocked and hopelessly unpersuasive.

"You saw the paper," he said. "There's a lot of the story in there, but it's confusing. That's always the problem. I could have pled out and got years, not life, but I didn't want to do that, I didn't want to lie. My own attorney told me we should just go ahead, go to trial, say the truth, but the truth was too confusing. Many people in here have that story. Many people in here had the same problem in one form or another."

"But if you weren't involved, it's not confusing, it's simple."

"There's nothing simple in the legal system. You know that. Especially not when you're a young man who looked like I did."

I hadn't told him anything about myself yet. I hadn't mentioned my reason for being there, or raised the possibility that I wasn't precisely the kind of person I might look like I was. There were obvious differences between us, and beneath them there were hidden, more mysterious differences, but there were also things we both understood. I don't want to sound wistful, but I think part of what kept us talking was that the fundamental problem of what we didn't and couldn't know was understood.

He had a tattoo on the inside of his forearm, dark green against his brown skin. It was a Star of David, or at least it was a six-pointed star, and because I wanted to change the subject, I asked him about it. I wondered if it was a Rastafarian symbol, knowing his Caribbean background, but he said no, it was a Theosophical symbol. He'd studied Theosophy in Angola, among other things, in his nine years there. The tattoo represented the male principle in balance with the female principle, one triangle for each. It was also a Seal of Solomon, he said, used to drive away demons. The biblical King Solomon had worn a ring with the symbol, half of it made of brass, half of iron; he signed commands to the good spirits with the brass side, to the evil spirits with the iron. I wrote all this in my notebook—*star of David tattoo is really Theosophy, 2 pyramids joined, Male/Female, good/evil, Eileen Baker in Pasadena, CA, was Theosophy instructor for K., Theos Society gives free books to inmates*—glad to have moved on to something other than the story of what had brought him here.

"I don't know how you deal with the day-to-day of this place," I said.

"There are ways."

"Bible study."

"You asked if they coerced me, the police, yeah, of course they coerced me. They had me detained for almost ten hours. There's nothing to eat, no one to talk to, even when you tell them what they want, they put you in handcuffs. 'You saw this, right? Isn't it true that so-and-so pulled a gun?' They put photos in front of you, leave you alone with photos of some-one's head blown open. They do that for ten hours. Say they know you're guilty, they have witnesses saying you're guilty. Then it's, 'We can make it easy for you, or we can make it hard for you.' It's not torture, but it's a kind of torture."

"So you said what?"

"I said what I had to say. That's what people do. That's what everyone does."

They were rehearsing the crucifixion scene behind us as we spoke. The previous night I'd had thick dreams that left me disoriented and vaguely anxious, and now before me, as in one of those dreams, a group of four men in oversized white T-shirts was overseeing the torture of a man play-ing Jesus whom they led down a staircase toward the cross. Seventy or so onlookers were pretending to weep or jeer or stare in awe. One of the prison guards was laughing at some-thing in the distance. My escort was, as usual, not around, though she was supposed to be monitoring my questions. I wasn't supposed to be asking questions about the inmates' cases. I watched as Jesus, now bearing the wooden cross, was hounded around the dusty arena by a mob of persecutors casting fake stones. On the dirt mound to one side, the two other crosses had already been raised up on their hinges and two other men playing thieves had been strung up, sagging there from the gibbets.

"Imagine that you're in a barn," Kendrick was saying now. *Now imagine that the barn is on fire ...*

He was being pulled away to go rehearse—along with his bit part in the play, he was one of the singers in the chorus, the Shepherds. I was a little relieved that we could stop talking for a while. As we both moved farther into the arena, toward those three crosses on their mound of dirt, he asked me if I'd call his mother when I got back to New Orleans. I wrote her number down in my notebook and told him I'd think about it. Or maybe I didn't even say I'd think about it. Maybe I just said I would, or at least that I'd try.

I saw Deborah sitting at a picnic table near some inmates beneath a huge plastic tent as I stood in the line for lunch. She looked exhausted, her sunglasses on, not even noticing me. I said before that I could hardly get away for a drink of water or a trip to the bathroom, and that was true in one sense, but in another sense, it could not have been true because I sometimes managed to sneak away for a few moments of privacy, smoking a cigarette outside the arena, alone, trying to absorb what I'd heard. There was a blue brick cube designated INMATE RESTROOM, all of its walls decorated with a cartoon of a po-faced convict in prison stripes, a ball and chain around his ankle. There were boarded-up concessions stands for the rodeo:

Camp "C" Concept Club
Boiled peanuts $3.00
Hog cracklins $5.00
Pig tails $1.00

Lunch was a pile of gluey rice with yellow gravy and some starchy vegetable the same color. Deborah had been joined by a few women prisoners when I sat down with her. They were talking about St. Gabriel, where in the past Deborah had been to shoot pictures on Mardi Gras and Halloween, the women in costumes, and on Christmas, when their children came to visit the decorated prison. The budget had been slashed since then—no more Mardi Gras, Christmas scaled back to almost nothing. One of the women said that last year all the kids received the same boxed Christmas gift: a ball, a tiny toy truck, a plastic cup. Her son had looked at the cup in particular and said, "It's a cup," uncertain as to how it could be construed as a gift. "Why can't they give one Xbox game for the same money?" she asked, for she knew that her son had understood the stigma of the cup.

I was seated a little ways down, across from a woman named Mary Bell, who was pretty and who was being eyed this whole time by virtually every man under that huge plastic tent. She was sending out secret gazes to a million points behind me, very discreetly, her eye movements almost undetectable, though she was constantly looking, constantly smiling. I don't think I've ever seen a face move the way Mary Bell's face was moving that day, taking in all that attention after so long with no attention.

I'd been hungry, but now, after eating about half of my food, I was sated, overly full, though I felt ashamed at not being able to finish. There was the pile of rice, gravy, that colorless vegetable. The inmates left, their plates clean. I looked back over my notebook at what Kendrick had just told me and I thought about telling it all to Deborah, but every time I recounted such stories they lost their weightiness and became mere anecdotes. Instead, I put my pen away and looked back down at my plate.

"My next project," Deborah said, "is kittens. Color photos of kittens."

"You're tired of despair?"

"Kitties in sweaters. Santa suits."

"There's always hopelessness. You could try that."

"How do you like it so far? Are you adapting to prison life?"

"I don't think so. I think I'm at a total loss so far."

She smiled, her eyes hidden by her sunglasses. "Well, that doesn't sound very good."

That night, I stayed up until two o'clock while Deborah slept, transcribing the day's notes onto my laptop. Most of them would be meaningless after twenty-four hours, single words that triggered paragraphs of associations as I typed them out. When I finished, I did another Internet search of "Kendrick King" and found the old *Times-Picayune* article, then I pulled up a court record that was eight pages of blurry single-spaced text. After five hours of transcribing the

shorthand in my notebook, I couldn't penetrate much of the
court document. There were two other people, a man and a
woman, who were almost certainly involved in the murder
that Kendrick was imprisoned for, but what Kendrick's role
in it all was I still couldn't say. I went outside for a cigarette
break and the cigarette break reminded me of freedom—I
knew it was a cliché, but I felt it powerfully. I was free to
think about Kendrick's case or not to, though that wasn't
really true: I kept thinking about it. Above me, the night sky
was full of stars—Orion, the hunter, and a white moon like
a desiccated slice of lime.

That whole week, Deborah and I didn't talk much about
why we were there, though we spent a lot of time together
when we weren't working—driving to dinner, having a
drink in our rooms. It was as if to put in words what we
were investigating would dissolve whatever it was we were
both privately trying to see. I was trying to see everything
clearly, but I realize that I missed at least as much that week
as I took in. On the morning of the first dress rehearsal, for
example, they were all getting their costumes on in the war-
ren of livestock chutes beneath the arena's grandstand—I
remember that. I remember Vernon "Vicious" Washington,
the superheavyweight boxing champion of Angola, walking
comically out of the makeshift dressing room in full biblical
dress and a white headwrap, but no shoes on his enormous
dust-covered feet. ("They run off with the props," he'd said,
explaining the lack of sandals.) I remember the actress who

was playing Mary being nearly thrown off the back of the donkey, who it turned out had not been quarantined after all and who was braying with a rich, horn-like call that sounded like a Jewish shofar, only louder. I hadn't been able to figure out who was blowing a horn until I finally went out to look and saw it was the donkey, bucking and rearing, the actress trying to hold on in her biblical tunic and veil, her posture one of helpless resignation. I remember that after everyone was dressed, there was this poignant vision: a long queue of men in one chute, a long queue of women in another, separated by brown bars, waiting for the sound technicians to fit them with their microphones, while in their outlandish costumes they talked in pairs across the bars all down the line—one-to-one, man-to-woman, without exception—as if involved in some sort of Bible-themed speed dating. It reminded me of Mary Bell at lunch the other day, sending those almost imperceptible smiles to the men behind me. I remember an excitement and focus to those conversations that was reminiscent of high school. I remember all that, but what I missed was some fracas in the distance, a scuffling that was over almost as soon as it began. I learned later what it was. It was two actors, a man and woman, who'd been detained by the guards for embracing each other too long. I heard a rumor later that they were husband and wife.

So you see, I often missed what really happened, even as I was trying my best to assess everything for what it really was.

•

I found Kendrick two mornings later behind the arena, barefoot and in the hooded robe that was his costume, sipping coffee by himself on a wooden bench. It was not just the monk-like robe that made him look baleful—his mood that day was different, menacing and closed off. It seemed to take him a few seconds to even recognize me. He looked off to one side, down a line of large blue plastic barrels full of bottled water, perhaps ashamed of some things he'd told me earlier. The day before, he'd claimed that he knew who'd really committed the murder he was incarcerated for: it was a young man who was only twenty at the time. He said that he would never divulge the man's name, that he couldn't put someone like that in prison, even if it meant getting out himself—he knew too much now about what it was like here, no one deserved to be in a place like this. He shared this with me on a set of crowded bleachers, in everyone's view (in prison, unless you're in solitary confinement, there's almost never any privacy), and he looked straight into my eyes, his own eyes moistening in urgency and embarrassment by the end. He looked straight ahead at nothing for a while, then finally raised his chin at another inmate, not in friendship or greeting but in something like simple acknowledgment. It occurred to me that life there was an unending performance shaped by the constant gazes of other people. It was impossible to know what to believe. Self-deprecation, self-awareness, ironic distance—these traits of sincerity can be faked but can they be faked beyond detection? If Kendrick was a liar, then he practiced the art of lying at a preternaturally subtle level that I've seldom seen matched in any other art form, which is to say that the performance contained no trace of artifice.

It was the day of the first performance when I found him on that bench in his robe with his coffee. Along with his costume, he was wearing a wristwatch he liked to wear, its band a braid of white plastic, its thickly bezeled face vaguely nautical. I asked him if his mother was coming— there was a free bus from New Orleans he'd mentioned before—but he said he didn't think so, he hadn't heard from her, things were not good for him right now.

"I ain't seen my daughter in nine years," he said then. "She's twelve now. You have kids?"

"No."

"No kids?"

"We didn't want any. It was by choice."

He became scientifically neutral, assessing this. "I was hoping my daughter would come out today," he said.

"I'm sorry."

"I know you can't do nothing for me. I understand that. You're not a lawyer. That's not why you're here."

He said he was done with the courts anyway, done with filing briefs—his appeals process had been exhausted years ago. He said that his one hope now was that someday he might get legal asylum in Saint Lucia, his mother's birth country, where he qualified for citizenship. That was his last chance—if they weren't going to give him parole, then maybe they'd at least let him go to Saint Lucia, where his family came from.

I said I hoped so. *I hope so.* I meant it in good faith, but given where we were it was impossible to say it without at least a trace of bad faith.

I wrote down his DOC number in my notebook and said I'd send him a letter when I got back to New Orleans. I didn't know yet that he wouldn't be permitted to receive it.

The day of that first performance was bleak, the sky the color of soot, the forecast predicting storms. There were maybe a hundred and fifty of us in the audience, about two thirds of whom were inmates, watching in the cold as a line of actors and actresses in shepherd's robes, including Kendrick, took their places in the center of the arena. Their garments were sand-colored, with rope belts and hoods that resembled those of desert saints in some early Renaissance painting. They began singing some minor-key phrases, their voices dirgelike and plush, a sound of grief, and before they could finish the first verse the sky erupted in a heavy rain that engulfed them. From my place in the grandstand, the downpour was like a white scrim obscuring everything before me. Beneath the awning, out of the weather, an inmate was doing sign language to a group of fellow inmates who were deaf. The narrator was delivering a prologue, telling us that his name was Luke, that he was there to tell us the story of our dear Lord and Savior, Jesus Christ, while across the aisle from me a woman who must have been an inmate's mother held up a digital camera, as if by continuing to film the play she could prevent it from being canceled. The singers' voices were beautiful and they were beautiful in their beige and white biblical costumes, but the rain was so strong that you could hardly pay attention to anything else. The Virgin Mary hunkered in her salmon tunic as the archangel Gabriel announced to her that she would soon have a miraculous child. Despite the rain, the actors were staying in character—it was what they were there to demonstrate, their ability to maintain self-discipline—but it seemed almost certain that they would have to call the play off in another minute or two.

As if in response, the Shepherds broke into full-fledged song, a gospel standard in a minor key called "Mary, Did You Know?" They had worked out the harmonies themselves, wide, surprising chords that flirted with the edges of atonality, Kendrick's deep bass undergirding it all. *Mary, did you know, the blind will see, the deaf will hear, the dead will live again.* Their singing was almost casual in its flawlessness, even as the rain lashed down on them. The juxtaposition of those two facts seemed to suggest that this situation was not so different from any other day in their unluxurious lives.

I saw the play many times, but in that first performance, begun in the heavy rain, something happened that reason tells me was mere coincidence but that the spirit of the day made seem uncanny. It was still raining. John the Baptist had just been charged with blasphemy, a mob had formed, and at the moment they were about to attack him John looked up and saw Jesus approaching in the distance. It was His first entrance. Suddenly the rain stopped—it didn't wane, it ceased completely. It was implausible how tranquil the weather became at the moment He appeared. The sudden lull resulted in a chorus of birdsong—so many birds started singing at once that you could barely hear Jesus' first words over the PA system. John baptized Him in an artificial oasis, then the actor playing Jesus did something I hadn't seen in rehearsals, so it surprised me. He pulled from beneath his green robe a live dove he'd been hiding in his hand. When he released it, it flew out above the grandstand—all those singing birds and then a live dove escaping from His robe.

I hope so, I'd told Kendrick about his dream of asylum in Saint Lucia.

I hope so.

It's easy to lose track of yourself. I don't mean in an existential way, I mean in a way that impinges on other people's lives.

2

Guineps—those big vines of grapelike fruit whose thick skin you peel back to reveal the delicately flavored plum-like innards. The carnival parade in Crown Heights, the beef patties and the colorful flags of the different islands, the soca music and the reggae. It was these seemingly trivial things we'd made small talk about that now revealed their enormous importance.

The story was "too confusing," Kendrick had said. When I got back to New Orleans, it occurred to me how susceptible I'd been to that phrase, "too confusing," how credulous I'd been about his claim that he was innocent. It was one of the reasons I felt trepidation about calling his mother, though I'd told him I'd try to do that. What I mean is that I didn't know if my credulity was anything more than soft-heartedness. It also made me uncomfortable to discover, after returning from Angola, that in some way I had been perceiving Kendrick's story as a version of my father's story. *It was something out of a movie—not even a realistic movie,*

I'd written about the aftermath of my father's murder. *There was the grief over the young man they'd all had a special liking for, and then there was the sense that his death would never seem real, that the sudden violence was so incongruous with his personality that the two could not be held in the mind at the same time.* I saw that I could have used some of these same words to describe my impression so far of Kendrick. It was complicated ("too complicated"). The word *death*, of course, would have to be replaced with *incarceration*. The connection was the word *incongruous*, the way that what had happened in both my father's life and Kendrick's seemed unrelated to who they seemed to be as people. I tried to explain some of this to Kendrick's mother, Sonia, when we finally spoke on the phone, but the phone made it hard to discuss anything very seriously, and so we decided to meet in person near where she worked, up the river from New Orleans in Ascension Parish, for her schedule was too busy to meet anywhere else.

I took I-10 toward Baton Rouge, past the airport, the suburbs, the long stretch of Lake Pontchartrain, then the Atchafalaya Swamp with the bony gray trunks of bald cypresses piercing through the bright green tupelos. It was not an unpleasant drive, but it was long enough that Sonia often slept between her shifts at the house of a coworker friend. She was a lab technician for a petrochemical company, working twelve-hour stretches that for four weeks were in the daytime and for the next four weeks in the night. She'd been a bank teller for several years, she'd told me on the phone, but after Katrina that job had disappeared, so now she commuted to this lab almost two hours from home,

occasionally supplementing the income she made there
by cleaning houses back in New Orleans so she could buy
Kendrick clothes and send him money for extra food from
the commissary and also so she could afford to visit him.
I got off the interstate and the industrial corridor began—
fertilizers, reagents, vinyl, polyethylene. I thought of the
brief, inadequate note I'd sent to Kendrick a few days before, one of a series of thank-you cards I'd written to the
people I'd interviewed, placing them in little envelopes that
I left unsealed so they could be screened by the prison administrators. Having stuffed these cards into a manila envelope, I sent them to the assistant warden, Cathy, asking her
to please distribute them for me. She'd told me the administration wanted to keep "all interaction between [me] and
the inmates under its supervision." If I wanted to go back
and do more interviews, then I couldn't write letters—the
administration would not "support pen pal relationships."

> Dear Kendrick,
>   Thank you for talking to me the other week. I hope we
> can follow up more sometime soon. You were one of the first
> people to give me his story and I will always be grateful for
> what you told me. In the meantime, I still like conch, even if
> you St. Lucians prefer to call it lambi.

About two miles down Ashland Road, I came upon
the main Shell plant, acres of depopulated furnaces, stor-
age tanks, metal tubes, scaffolding, pipes—the illegible
machinery of ethylene manufacturing—the vast sprawl of

it reminiscent of Angola. (I learned later that like Angola it had been built on a former slave plantation.) I got lost somewhere on the river levee and had to check the map on my phone, then called Sonia for directions. There were a few cattle in the fields, most of the houses in ruins, the rest an agglomeration of trailers or plain wooden shacks. There was a church with three crosses in front made of rusted sheet metal attached to iron scaffolding, the sheet metal torn away in shreds. I eventually found Sonia's friend's house down another road, beyond a gas station and store, the Yousef Quick Stop. When she opened the door, she was dressed in a pale blue lab coat, and she kept talking with someone on her cell phone as she showed me in. The house had a purplish gray sectional sofa and a flat-screen TV that was turned up so loud I didn't know how she could have been having a phone conversation over it. It gradually occurred to me that she was so accustomed to having the TV on that it didn't register to her that it was actually on.

"I told you Girl Ville, Girl Ville," she said after she hung up.

"You're right, I know," I said. "I didn't understand."

She was saying "Carville," not "Girl Ville"—Carville was the town we were in. I hadn't been able to make out this simple statement over the phone because of her Saint Lucian accent. I looked at the living room, which had the sterility of a model home, or perhaps more aptly of some of the guest facilities I'd seen at Angola. Sonia had been washing some spare lab coats in the laundry off the kitchen and now, as she went to put them in the dryer, she asked if

I wanted anything to drink but I told her no, I'd brought some mineral waters for us—they were in my bag, along with my notebook and pen and a copy of the book I was planning to give her, my book about my father. It was, of course, what had led me here, as I'd explained when we first talked on the phone, telling her the story of my connection to Deborah and how it had brought us together to the passion play at Angola. Sonia had remarked on the element of fate in all this, though I was still reluctant to look at it that way, to feel grandiose in that way. Like many people, she didn't know what to say about my book when I presented it to her. We were back in the living room, sitting on the sofa, the mineral waters on the coffee table before us, and she held the book in her hands like a family album, as if trying to take in what it must mean to me. To suggest we might have something in common because of my father's death felt slightly wrong to me, but I also felt I had to explain again why I was there. Tears had started to well at the edges of her eyes when I mentioned Kendrick, the tears distorted and accentuated by the fact that she was dressed for work in her boxy coat. I thought of her son, his "Weimaraner eyes," as Deborah had called them, and I remembered something I'd written in the book Sonia was now holding: *My father could be quiet. There was something he held in reserve, a mystery about him, even a romance, but there wasn't crookedness, there wasn't criminality.* The connection I kept seeing between Kendrick and my father gave me an uncomfortable sense of distance from the moment I was in now, as if I were watching Sonia and myself on a screen, insufficiently attentive to the fact that in her mind her son was the victim of the most horrible injustice. She placed the book on the sofa beside her, then reached for a tissue from the box on the coffee table. I told her we didn't have to do this if she didn't want to, but she said no, she wanted to, and when I asked if she was sure, she recoiled slightly, as if a little indignant that I didn't understand.

"I invited you here," she said. "Not many people ever asked me about this. I invited you because it's good to talk."

She showed me a Polaroid of her and Kendrick taken at the prison on his last birthday, standing with their arms around each other before a painted backdrop of a waterfall surrounded by steep mountains with rounded crests like those in China. She looked completely different in the picture, dressed in a neat beige suit with pearl earrings, rings on her fingers, her hair and makeup freshly done. Kendrick, in a white T-shirt and jeans, peered into the camera with the solemn pride of a figure in a nineteenth-century daguerreotype. She told me a little about what their visits involved, saying that it wasn't like in the movies—they sat at tables in chairs, not in those booths with phones separated by glass. They were able to hug each other, kiss each other, to interact like a normal mother and son. She even smiled slightly when she began to describe the food she could order for them—pizza, barbecue chicken, jambalaya, po'boys. When they ran out of things to say, she told me, which could happen because she often spent the whole day there, six or seven hours, there were TVs they could watch, and if people brought kids there were coloring books and even video games for them to play.

"I'm coping," she told me. "There's times when I don't have enough money to send, and I tell him I'm sorry, I know you need food, but it's either food or I keep coming to visit. One or the other. It's hard on him, I know. He lost some weight last time. I could see that he lost it."

We sat in silence for a while, then she asked me if my mother was still alive. This question always surprises me, though I've heard it many times. I said yes, and she asked another question people often do, was my mother okay?, and I told her yes, it was a long time ago. She had remarried, we had moved to another city, she and my stepfather were still together.

"We talked about a lot of heavy things when I was writing my book," I said. "I didn't really remember my father, even though I should have—I was six when he died, old enough to have memories. But it was a blank spot for me, who he was, so I liked talking to my mother about it, even though it was hard for her. I maybe take things too seriously sometimes, to the point that it's a little ridiculous. Maybe there's something wrong with me, wanting to keep having conversations like that."

We looked at each other as if to acknowledge that what I'd just said was a little absurd, though this acknowledgment somehow also seemed to imply the opposite: that we understood each other enough now to be able to speak frankly. She told me then that a few days ago she'd learned that the kidney disease she'd had for several years had progressed to the point where she needed treatment. This was what she'd meant before when she'd said she was "coping," that in fact she didn't feel well most of the time. She hadn't told Kendrick about this, and she asked me not to tell him either, though I'd explained to her that I couldn't communicate with him anyway. She was hoping that her other son, Marcus, might be able to come stay with her for a while when she started dialysis treatments. He lived in New York, and she knew he couldn't stay forever, but she didn't know what else to do. She told me then that Kendrick had been difficult before the play, that he had somehow gotten it into his mind that his twelve-year-old daughter, Aysha, might be able to come to the prison to see him perform, though neither he nor Sonia had had any contact with Aysha in many years. She said she'd stayed in touch with Aysha's mother, Janelle, for a short time after Kendrick went to prison, but after Katrina everyone had scattered, and now she didn't even know where they lived. One of the last times she'd seen Aysha was at the trial, she said—Aysha crying for her father, Sonia and Janelle telling her he would come home soon, lying to her in that way because that was the only thing one could do.

"She was finally getting to be a talker," she said. "She'd been slow learning how to talk before, but she had it by then. With her, it was like silence, silence, silence, then all the sudden—full sentences."

She was three, the last time she'd seen her father, I thought. Kendrick was twenty-two—a part of him was still twenty-two, it occurred to me, still referring when we met nine years later to rappers and basketball stars that no one had talked about much in those nine years.

I asked her if Kendrick had ever had any trouble with the law before he was arrested that summer, and she said no, that in fact he'd had "a lot of friends who were police." I didn't know what to say to that. It was the first time I doubted anything she'd told me, though I believed she believed it herself. She went on to tell me that the summer Kendrick was arrested he was planning to become an EMT, because he wanted to "help people." He'd gone back to community college and was planning to transfer to a four-year school, because that was "the caliber of person" he intended to be. I'd told her on the phone that I had no plans to write about any of this, though I'd also said that I never knew what I was going to write until I was actually writing it. Deborah made images—their value was obvious. The value of writing seemed far less obvious to me, just a groping around in the unknowable. As Sonia told me a story now about Kendrick learning to speak Spanish as a child, so that he could make friends with some neighborhood kids who only spoke Spanish, I thought that at least some of this had to be just sentimental exaggeration, but I didn't press her. I remembered that day at the prison when Kendrick had told me that he knew who really committed the murder but that he would never divulge the other man's name. I remembered the way he'd tried not to cry without trying too hard—the embarrassment of the effort, his fear of seeming too performative.

The night of his arrest, Sonia told me now, two detectives from the sheriff's office had come by her house—they were looking for Kendrick as a potential witness, they said,

and they left her their business card. When Kendrick came
home a few hours later, he went to the detective bureau to
clear things up, but he was gone a long time—it was four or
five the next morning when the police car returned, pulling
into Sonia's driveway in the dark. It was summertime, hot,
but she remembered that her hands went numb, she got so
cold. They had come to pick up a pair of Kendrick's basketball shoes, the detective said. They were bright green,
she remembered—like all his shoes they were immaculately
clean. A forensics team later tested the shoes for bloodstains but found no bloodstains. She said that not long before all this, she happened to have served on a jury in the
same courthouse in which Kendrick would eventually face
trial, and she remembered how the sight of all those young
men in handcuffs had affected her. It was disorienting to
remember now, like déjà vu, as if everything since had been
just an illusion, or some sort of amnesia. They wouldn't let
Kendrick out of the car that night. They wouldn't let her
speak to him. It was the last time she ever saw him outside a
courtroom or a prison, standing there shivering in the heat,
looking at him through the window of the police car.

"I thought about calling 'On Your Side,'" she said, referring to a public advocacy segment on the local TV news. She
looked at me as if to see if I thought this was a good idea,
something to pursue possibly even now. She told me then
that a friend of hers had been at a beauty parlor recently,
and there she had come across a woman who had made a
statement to the police about Kendrick all those years ago,
though she never testified at his trial. This woman had been

a suspect in the murder herself, but she negotiated a plea deal and so she was free. Sonia's friend had overheard this woman saying that there was a man in Angola doing time for a murder he'd had nothing to do with.

I brought up the Innocence Project of New Orleans, which offers free legal assistance to inmates who are serving life sentences or death sentences and who claim to have been falsely convicted. But as I wrote down the information and tore the sheet out of my notebook, I also remembered the caveats on IPNO's website:

Please understand that we receive a large number of letters every week and it will take some time for us to respond to the application or inquiry.

Please tell your loved one to be patient. It often takes years before we can begin to review a case.

Do not call our office to inquire about the status of an application. *We do not have the staff to handle phone calls and they only slow down our review of applications.*

"I brought you all the way out here on a Sunday," she said, after dabbing at her eyes with another tissue, for she'd started crying again. I didn't know what she meant at first, and she just shook her head, not telling me, as if resigned to the idea that I wouldn't accept her meaning anyway. Sunday, I realized—the day of prayer. She was not at church but in Carville, in this house that wasn't hers, microwaving meals she stockpiled at the dollar store, she'd told me earlier, between shifts at the lab. Her tears were tears of near hopelessness, made bearable by faith. Perhaps it was in some way a relief for her to talk to someone, as she'd said, but I couldn't know. She thanked me in any case. She said the next time we'd have to meet at her "real house," back in New Orleans, the house she'd bought several years ago that would one day go to her sons, including Kendrick, "as soon as he comes home."

I picked up my bag to leave and we hugged and I said I'd stay in touch. She stood at the opened door as I walked down the driveway toward my car—I looked back, more than once, and saw that she was still standing there before the empty house, watching as I got into the driver's seat. I waved at her a last time before I started the engine, then backed down the driveway. She didn't stop looking until I was gone.

When I got home, I went online and printed out the long summary of Kendrick's hearing before the U.S. District Court of Appeals, which was the most complete account of his case I could find at that point. The document was so confusing that I made a diagram of all the names of the people involved. I still couldn't quite figure out how Kendrick fit into the mosaic of names. I looked them all up on the Internet, hoping for more clues, but almost none of them had a profile beyond some street addresses and phone numbers. Nothing on Janelle Bryers, the mother of Kendrick's daughter, Aysha—not even an address. Nothing on his father, Donovan King, who Kendrick had told me now lived in Maryland.

Later, Sonia texted me a photo, a copy of the Polaroid of

her and Kendrick posed before that painted backdrop of the waterfall and mountains. It occurred to me then that I didn't know what the murder victim, Damien Martin, looked like. I only knew what Kendrick looked like, Kendrick and his mother, Sonia. I realized that this in itself was an enormous distortion in the way I was perceiving this story.

3

When I got out of bed, my wife, Sarah, was sleeping. I could see even in the darkness the pair of barrettes, covered in gold glitter and shaped like butterflies, that she kept fixed to the shade of her bedside lamp. She was an obstetrician and gynecologist, and sometimes I dreamed about having to do her job, standing in the delivery room with mask and gloves on and no idea of how to proceed. Every time I saw those barrettes on her lamp, I remembered a trip we'd made to Costa Rica where we'd seen enormous butterflies six inches wide, their wings an implausibly brilliant blue. At one point during that trip, we'd taken a six-hour horseback ride over mountains and across rivers. There was a steep rocky gorge that the horses plunged down at full speed, and I remember looking back, seeing my wife assume an instinctive pose of balance, one hand holding the reins while the other extended high in the air behind her head, whooping with fear and laughter but also achieving perfect rodeo form. I had the kind of temperament that sometimes caused me to wake up in the middle

of the night like this, my mind turned away from such pleas-
ant memories. I went into the room now where I worked and
took out one of the banker's boxes stuffed full of documents
I'd amassed while researching my book about my father's
murder. I hadn't opened it in at least four years, and I was surprised by the dense profusion of its contents—folders full of
newspaper clippings, FBI transcripts, photographs, rubber-
banded stacks of notecards. There were the photocopied articles about the land business my father had been a part of for
several years, the hundreds if not thousands of pages I'd read
and reread. In 1975, my father was murdered when he had to
testify against his former business partner in a probe that exposed an extensive pattern of bribery and fraud. More than
thirty years later, I'd tried to understand why this had happened and why no one had ever been charged with, much less
convicted of, my father's killing. *Grand Jury Witness*, read the
first headline in the pile, *Is Slain Gang Style*. I found the clip-
ping but saw that the photograph of my father's dead body
had been whited out, which was strange, because I knew I'd
seen it somewhere. I could remember the way the picture
had been bleached by the microfiche machine, softened into
an image of a man younger than I was, lying in a parking
garage stairwell, his eyes closed, dressed in a suit, as if he'd
fallen asleep there for some reason on his way to a wedding.
It was four o'clock in the morning. I couldn't stop looking for
the picture, knowing it was somewhere in the folder. "You're
pressing the button," my friend Simeon would say later, referring to this kind of compulsion. George Orwell, writing
about why he wrote, said that "one would never undertake

such a thing if one were not driven on by some demon one can neither resist nor understand." I finally found the photograph toward the back of the stack.

It was late, a different weeknight, but the bar was close to home, nearly empty, and we liked to go there for the music. The singer had a voice that might have made him famous fifty years ago. He was a little paunchy now, graying, flourishing a white handkerchief he sometimes used to dab his forehead, singing a song about surviving, enduring. The drummer stayed just behind the beat so that the slow song had kick, the guitar player melting little country-and-western riffs into soul. It sounded like it was 1970 and instead of seven of us in the bar who knew some of the words it was a theater and there were many more of us. The world outside was on fire, it always was, and though the singer didn't sing about any of that he alluded to it in the timbre of his voice. He sang about coming home to New Orleans— parochial, poor, beautiful, inescapable—and the part of the song that was celebratory was not false and the part that was sad was not weak. Sarah always liked the way his belly moved when he danced. I liked the sound of his band in this bar, linoleum on the floor, the low stage, the bulky metal chairs painted black, the song about a moment like this—the smoke, the liquor, the colored lights, time stolen from work and worry, not just surviving but something more than that, something that made you smile and cry at the same time.

4

I eventually saw a photograph of Damien Martin, the murder victim, about a month later, when I went with Deborah to the Old Records Office of the Jefferson Parish Clerk of Courts. I'd been spending a lot of time there reading Kendrick's case file—"pressing the button," as Simeon had said, driven on by some demon. At the Old Records Office, there turned out to be almost thirty photographs of Damien Martin, glossy 8-by-10 color prints, kept in a manila envelope in a cardboard box amid shelves and shelves of other evidence from other investigations. The photos were presented to us at a table by a sheriff's deputy, who sat there silently as Deborah and I looked at them under fluorescent lights. There was a large blowup of Damien Martin's bare foot on a backdrop of blue vinyl, the skin wrinkled and sere, a tag bearing his name and address and case number strung from the big toe. There was a gruesome picture of Martin's head resting on a blood-soaked cloth laid atop a plastic sheet, a stream of blood issuing from his nostrils, his eyes blurry

slits, maroon-colored spatters on his cheeks and nose. There
were more than a dozen close-ups of the bullet wounds to
his forehead, temple, and ear (small round seeping holes),
and close-ups of the tattoos on his forearms (the name Katy,
a cross surmounted by four stars). There were pictures of
him sprawled dead on a table in the coroner's office, still in
a black Karl Kani T-shirt and black jeans, and there were
pictures of his body in those same clothes on the linoleum
floor in the kitchen at Athena Street, lying beside a bucket of
joint compound and a mop in a plastic pail. There was a picture of Martin still alive, his two young daughters sitting on
his lap, white ribbons in their hair, Martin in a gray sweater
and an Adidas cap, his daughters in matching sweatshirts
with giraffes on them, both smiling, one with a mix of missing teeth, baby teeth, and adult teeth, the younger one with
almost no teeth yet at all. The deputy pulled more objects
out of the cardboard box. There was a smaller manila envelope, this one containing the bullet fragments retrieved from
the scene. He handed the envelope to me—I could feel the
metal bundled tightly inside the thick paper—before I could
think to refuse. He pulled out Martin's black bucket hat,
kept as evidence because it had a bullet hole in it where the
crown met the brim, the edges of the tear stained brown as if
singed. In the stack of photographs, I now saw, were several
pictures of the hat resting on the kitchen floor, a yellow plastic marker labeled "P" framing the perforation. I thought of
the smiling faces of Damien Martin's daughters in the family portrait. They would be adolescents now, and likely had
no idea that these artifacts of their father even existed.

There was no reason to do this work other than the need to do it, out of some untenable faith in your own way of seeing. Over the course of several days, I'd read through more than six hundred pages of court documents that detailed Kendrick's case, and I had been faced once again with the idea that he might simply be lying, that I had made a naïve mistake. That was why I'd asked the staff at the Old Records Office if I could get a transcript of the four taped statements he had made to the police. It turned out that I could not only get a transcript but could actually listen to the tapes themselves, the sound of the exact words in Kendrick's own voice. That was why Deborah and I were there. I'd wanted her to come because I wanted to see how she, an outsider, would interpret what we heard. I wanted to know if the part of me that still believed Kendrick might be innocent was simply deluded.

The deputy finally located the tapes in the box of evidence. I had the transcript before me, which I tried to place so that both Deborah and I could see it. The deputy loaded the first of four mini-cassettes into a small black dictation recorder, and I took out my notebook and pen and we began.

This is a taped statement of Kendrick Donovan King, K-I-N-G. Black male, date of birth 9/20/82, currently residing 700 Avenue F, Westwego, his mother's residence. Statement is being taken on August 30, 2003, at approximately 6:14 by Detective Ray Lagarde of Jefferson Parish Sheriff's

Office Homicide Division in reference to item
F-94857-02.

LAGARDE: Mr. King, uh, is it not in fact true that,
oh, maybe twenty minutes ago, sometime before
6:00 p.m. on this date, you called the detective bureau, looking for me?

KING: Yes.

LAGARDE: Okay, and what caused you to do that?

KING: Well, because my mother had called me and
told me that two detectives had come by the house.
She said you gave her your card, so I called you right
away.

LAGARDE: And so, after a brief conversation, we
came back here into this interview room.

KING: Yes, sir.

LAGARDE: And I said that this was in regard to
Damien Martin, who had been murdered the week
before.

KING: Yes.

LAGARDE: And I asked you if you knew him.

KING. Yes.

LAGARDE: And you indicated that you did know him.

KING: Yes.

LAGARDE: And I asked you if you had been around the building at all on the day of the murder, in the morning hours, in particular, on the day in question. If, you know, you could account for your whereabouts, during those morning hours. And what did you say?

KING: No, I wasn't there during the morning hours.

LAGARDE. Okay. That's right. You indicated that you were not there in the morning hours.

KING: That's right.

LAGARDE: And when you first told me that, only then did I start filling out this form I'm showing you now, entitled Jefferson Parish Sheriff's Office Rights of Arrestee or Suspect.

KING: Yes. That's correct.

As we listened, Martin's bucket hat, the envelope containing the bullet fragments, and the photographs of the crime scene were still on the table. I noticed that Deborah and I weren't looking at them. We were looking at the mini-cassette player, which sat at the center of everything with a strange, almost necromantic aura, transmitting these captured voices from ten years ago. Lagarde was reading Kendrick his Miranda rights now. It would have been the second time that evening that he had done so. He pointed out that Kendrick had already waived these rights and already initialed and signed a form to that effect. In less than half an hour, in other words, Kendrick had gone from being a potential witness to being a suspect. On the tape now, Kendrick agreed once again to the terms Lagarde repeated to him. *I understand what my rights are. I'm willing to make a statement and answer questions. I do not want a lawyer at this time. I understand and know what I'm doing.*

They resumed the narrative, Kendrick saying again that he wasn't at Martin's apartment building during the morning hours, that he was at his girlfriend Janelle Bryers's house, nine miles away. Janelle had taken their daughter, Aysha, to day care that morning, then gone to work, leaving him alone all day in Janelle's trailer house.

LAGARDE: And had anyone seen you between the time Janelle left for work that morning and when she returned home that night? Can anybody account for your whereabouts that day?

There was silence, then Lagarde reminded Kendrick that he was being recorded, and Kendrick began a blurry recollection of waking up that morning and calling a friend from Janelle's home phone. Lagarde listened—patient, not accusatory, just someone who wanted to get this task taken care of as quickly and efficiently as possible. He asked again if anyone had seen Kendrick, rather than just speaking to him on the phone, and Kendrick said, no, no one had actually seen him that day, not until Janelle came home a little after six o'clock. He had not gone anywhere else that day? No. He had stayed inside the trailer the whole time?

KING: Yes.

LAGARDE: All day long. Okay.

KING: Until six fifteen. Six thirty.

LAGARDE: Okay. Six fifteen. Six thirty. And where did you go then?

KING: I went to Athena Street.

Athena Street was the location of Damien Martin's apartment building. Kendrick's responses so far had been confident, eager, like someone answering quiz questions with impatient mastery, but now he began to rush, his voice deeper and louder.

LAGARDE: You went to Athena Street?

KING: Yes.

LAGARDE: You left your girlfriend's and the first place that you went was Athena Street.

KING: Yes.

LAGARDE: And why was that?

KING: I sometimes go to Athena to see friends.

LAGARDE: Friends?

KING: Yes.

LAGARDE: Okay. And who in particular were you going to see that night?

KING: Normal times, I had pulled into the second driveway. No ... you see, Athena. I always pull up there and, you know, just stand outside and holler to whoever it is to come outside.

LAGARDE: So on the day of the murder, you weren't going there to see anyone in particular? You just happened to go there?

KING: Yes.

LAGARDE. Okay. Uh, but that's when you discovered there'd been a shooting. A shooting involving Damien Martin?

KING: I seen Antoinette. She said Damien got shot. You know what I'm saying? He got shot! He got shot! I was coming out the car and I seen her. He got shot, you know? That's why I had walked through the police tape. I wasn't thinking. I saw Antoinette and I just walked through it.

LAGARDE: Now, who is Antoinette?

KING: Antoinette. She live next door to Damien.

LAGARDE: Okay.

KING: She said he got shot. He got shot. She walking up the street and I said, "Y'all, you know, where y'all was at? Y'all didn't see nothing?" She say, "Oh, we ain't even…" She said, "We ain't even…we was inside the apartment." She said they was inside, in the apartment next door, and all they heard was cabinets slamming. I said, "What? What you mean? Cabinets slamming?"

LAGARDE: They, we. Who? Who else was with Antoinette?

KING: Her boyfriend.

LAGARDE: Do you know her boyfriend's name?

KING: Yes. His name is Lawrence.

LAGARDE: Do you know his last name?

KING: No.

LAGARDE: Can you describe him for me?

KING: Short. Maybe five foot eight. Light skin, reddish hair.

LAGARDE: How is he built?

KING: Heavy. Heavy build. Got a . . . got a gunshot wound in his left leg.

LAGARDE: That's right. Okay, that's—that's a pretty accurate description of the person we're talking about. Let me ask you this, Kendrick. In all fairness before, I indicated to you that, you know, that several people had said you were on the grounds, uh, at Athena Street, at the time or around the time of the murder.

KING: Uh, huh.

LAGARDE: Is there any truth to that?

KING: No. No truth at all.

LAGARDE: No truth at all.

KING: No. No, sir.

LAGARDE: Okay. Had you ever been in Damien Martin's apartment before?

KING: Yes. About two months ago.

LAGARDE: And what was the purpose of that visit?

KING: Uh, Jodi. His baby mama, Jodi, has a little girl. Damien and Jodi has a baby, a little girl, and I wanted to see this little girl, 'cause my little girl is…like a few months older. And Jodi said her little girl ain't talking yet. She asked me if it was a problem. Because my little girl, she … she ain't talk till late, like she past two before she really start talking. So I said, no, I'll come and see her. So that's why I had come by there.

LAGARDE: To see Jodi's baby?

KING: Yes.

LAGARDE: Okay ... I just want to ask you. Were you aware of any illegal activity, any narcotics or anything, emanating from that apartment on Athena Street?

KING: No.

LAGARDE: You understand that's not the point of my investigation?

KING: Yes, sir.

LAGARDE: You understand that I'm a homicide detective. I'm simply interested in the murder of Damien Martin and not in any illegal activity that may have gone on prior to the murder.

KING: I understand.

LAGARDE: Your answer would still be the same.

KING: Yes.

It felt odd to talk in front of the deputy across the table from us, and Deborah and I didn't say anything after this first tape ended. We just waited as he rewound the cassette and put in the next one, after confirming we were ready for it. The next tape began the same way the first had, with Kendrick's name, race, date of birth, address. The date, though, had changed. It was 3:40 the next morning. More than nine hours had passed. There was nothing in Kendrick's voice that suggested abuse or duress, but he had been in the interview room all that time and the story he recounted now—calmly, pliantly, in the same tone as before—was entirely different. He said now that he had in fact been at Athena Street during the morning hours. He said that he and a man named Lawrence and a woman named Antoinette had decided to rob Damien Martin— they did this because they needed heroin. Kendrick and Lawrence went over to Martin's apartment, and when Lawrence ordered Kendrick to lock the door, things escalated. Kendrick went upstairs to search the rooms for money or drugs. While he was upstairs, he heard the first gunshot and turned back.

KING: He was on his knees, with his hands in the air. Pleading. Begging for his life.

LAGARDE: And then the other shots came.

KING: He slumped down after that. I mean, he was out.

LAGARDE: And what did you do at that point?

KING: I was just standing there. I was in shock. I was looking at Damien and Lawrence says, "Move, move. What you standing around for?" He opened the door. He went busting out through the door and I followed him.

LAGARDE: And what happened when you saw Antoinette?

KING: Lawrence told her what happened. He said, "I shot Damien." Antoinette, she said, "What? Why you shot Damien?" He said, "'Cause he seen my face."

LAGARDE: Okay.

KING: Lawrence, he sat down, it was like he was in shock. You know what I mean? He was like fuck it, I shot him. And Antoinette, she was scared. We was both scared, nervous. I just drove them where they wanted to go. They went inside his auntie's house. (*Sobbing.*) He took him a bath. And I left. And I came back later. Later that night.

LAGARDE: When the police were there?

KING: Yeah. About six thirty.

LAGARDE: To the scene of the crime.

KING: Yeah.

He was having trouble talking now, his speech broken by low moans. When the tape finished, the deputy explained that in an interrogation room the microphone is often affixed to the wall almost at the level of the table, much lower than you would expect, because when a suspect confesses, he's often bent over, speaking almost inaudibly. This was how Kendrick sounded toward the end of his interrogation. There were four tapes altogether, the last two very short. By the end, we'd been in the room with the deputy for about forty minutes, and Deborah and I still hadn't really talked.

LAGARDE: Okay. Is everything you've told me true and correct to the best of your knowledge?

KING: Yes, sir.

LAGARDE: Okay. And how do you feel you've been treated by me tonight, Kendrick?

KING: Fairly. Fair.

LAGARDE: Let me ask you one last question. Why did you want to participate in a crime like this?

KING: I was sick. I needed to get high. We was going to hit a lick.

LAGARDE: Hit a lick?

KING: Hoping to find drugs, money, whatever. I needed to get high. It's why I come back later that evening, because I still needed to get high.

From my reading of his case file, I knew a lot more about Kendrick's past than Deborah did. She had simply heard the four taped statements we'd just listened to. His defense at his trial was that the last three tapes were just a series of lies he'd recited under coercion from the police. I looked over at Deborah now and saw that she was focused not on what we'd just heard but on one of the photographs of Damien Martin. It was the one of Martin with his two daughters sitting on his knee, smiling at the person taking the picture—perhaps their mother, Jodi—in their matching sweatshirts with the giraffes on them. I looked at the picture and realized, again, how my focus on Kendrick had distorted my view of what had happened. It made me hesitant to ask Deborah what I had brought her there to ask her.

"He was desperate," she said, when I finally did.

I had believed he had nothing to do with the murder at all. When he first told me his story, I'd formed an impression of Kafkaesque randomness—*why had the police even considered him a suspect?*—and this impression had affected everything about my conversation with Sonia, I saw now. I didn't want to believe what I'd just heard Kendrick say on the last three tapes, but it didn't "sound" coerced, or like a lie. It hadn't sounded that way to Deborah, either. But what he'd said amounted to a confession of second-degree murder—in legal terms, in Louisiana, where just being present made him a participant—whether I agreed with that or not.

I tried to contact Kendrick's lawyer a few days later. I tried to contact the detective Ray Lagarde, who had interrogated him, and who no longer worked for the Jefferson Parish Sherriff's Office. I called and e-mailed them both, but as I expected, neither would talk to me.

I saw within myself a kind of ignorance that grew deeper the more I looked at it. I kept trying to understand what had happened in Kendrick's life. I kept trying to imagine it. All this started more than four years ago.

PART TWO

MIRAGE

5

A Monday in August, 2003. He pushes at the edge of the blackout curtain and sees how bright it is outside—kids' bikes, a plastic folding chair—all the trailer houses under the weed trees, the cars at random angles on the gravel shoulder. It's morning, he has time to follow through on the help-wanted ads, but he can hardly see now that he's looked out the window at the sunlight. He hears on the TV McDonald's celebrating Pixar's *Finding Nemo* with a new triple-thick shake you'll find sweet. Aysha's blocks are all over the floor. There are crayons and toys scattered over the plastic play mat. Dishes in the sink—sippy cups and plastic bowls and a million tiny colored spoons. Janelle's at work, Aysha at day care, he's alone. He thinks he can surprise them, put everything in its place, find a way to do that, it's Janelle's birthday, *Happy Birthday*, that's something he can do. *Caring. Discipline. Passion. Become a professional chauffeur with Envoy Limousine. Provide exceptional customer service while having fun.*

He tries to enter into the room's soft darkness, but something familiar and inclusive about the TV reminds him that he's only here because he has no money, no car, no one has called. Five days back after ten days in the parish jail, then the court appearance last Friday, waiting all morning with a can of Coke so they could schedule another hearing, more waiting. But then there was yesterday, that moment at the Oakwood mall outside Footaction when Janelle told him to wipe Aysha's face, *Clean up her face, Kendrick*, and he took the wipe and bent down over her in the stroller and saw her cheeks, her nose, so intricate and small she seemed to have been shaped from a mold, and that was good, his baby girl, he couldn't believe how it made him feel, even while some small part of him hung back, thinking how it looked. Aysha, Janelle—his girls. Going to the Oakwood mall with Aysha in his arms, her hair in pig tails and beads, Janelle trying on those shoes, suede straps latticed over her ankles. *Clean up her face, Kendrick*: it was not just bossing, it was a sign that he was welcome, that she felt comfortable enough to play it like everything was normal. He could make a few phone calls, then think about starting on the dishes, stop laughing at the the help-wanted ads. *Chauffeurs must be 24 or older, hold a valid Chauffeur's License or CDL with a "P" Endorsement, have a clean driving history, and excellent customer service skills.*

No one called him back. He couldn't call them anymore, he should not have called them before, but now he has to stay here in this trailer until Janelle comes home from work with the car, that's where he is. The AC in the window shudders out a thin breath of damp air and he can see the yellow glow of heat outside through the plastic accordion frame. He thinks of his old job stocking shelves at the Save-A-Lot, sitting in the break room—*I ran out of sick days, so I called in dead!*—smoking up outside the store, then the days in jail, a different kind of joke, carrying rolls of toilet paper everywhere he went because he kept shitting, retching, wiping his nose. He tells himself he's not going to get high, because he doesn't want to still be high in case somebody comes, if somebody calls, and now this is a loop he recognizes, foreseeing an outcome and resisting it, foreseeing it and denying it—Aysha is his child too, he needs to help more, man up, he knows that.

He remembers the lighted tier at night, the echoes of all those voices, how you could be scared and appalled and also want to laugh at the same time. In the mornings, you had to leave the cell and sit with everyone else, and at first he was so sick he could hardly move. Eleven dollars in his wallet now. A Quik Cash Lifetime Membership Card and a receipt from Cash America Pawn of New Orleans. He thinks of Janelle in a black T-shirt and sunglasses, Janelle and Aysha in the parking lot of the Oakwood mall walking slowly away from the car. It goes by like this, more time passing than he can understand.

Outside the building on Athena Street, there's a few people he knows, a kid with braids and camouflage shorts and no shirt, and a kid in an Atlanta Braves cap who sits in an old office chair on wheels left to disintegrate in the rain and

sun. He looks at the brickwork smudged black with mold
and knocks on Antoinette's door. She's short and heavy and
the room behind her seems absolutely dark because of the
blackout curtain pulled close up against the windows. She
still hasn't made eye contact with him, backing up slowly
into the apartment, and he follows her in, the living room
like the one in Janelle's trailer, except the floor is peeling
white linoleum instead of carpet, the TV, now that he's inside, casting a faint brown light on the furniture and the
dishes.

"I tried to call you but nobody picked up," he says. "It's
early. I know it's early. I was just sitting around pretending
to look at the paper."

"Lawrence ain't come home last night." She looks at him
steadily now, her eyebrows still. "He just called twenty minutes ago, said he by Andrea's house."

"Andrea?"

"My auntie."

"I know that. I just always wondered why you call her
Andrea if she's your auntie."

She's smoking now, her hand on the kitchen counter.
"She's just like that. She don't want to sound old, I guess."

They get high and watch a movie, an old one he saw
many times when he was a kid, though it's different now
from what he remembers. Once he's smoking he's thirsty no
matter how much he drinks, his hands wet from the con-
densation on his cup. He begins to notice how many times
people in the movie get shot by guns—Mossbergs, MAC-
10s, Calicos, a .44 Magnum, a silver Smith & Wesson with

black rubber grips. He wants to turn off the sound so he
doesn't have to hear the actors talking. He wants to be back
at Janelle's trailer, watching the movie by himself with the
sound off, some music on. Antoinette tells him she has to go
up into the bedroom to make a phone call. She has on black
sweatpants and a T-shirt and an unbelted beige robe. He
remembers now: Antoinette's auntie, Andrea. The apartment they're in—Antoinette's apartment—is really Andrea's.
Andrea is staying in Metairie these days. It's always confusing, who's doing what. Riding with his cousin Mason last
Friday after his court appearance, both of them high again,
running into Antoinette, all of that time going by, his face
shrunk further and further into the darkness, a flat, faint
image encased inside the glass of the window. He sits there
now in some of Mason's clothes. He looks taller than usual
because he shaved himself bald that Friday, his bare skull
gleaming like the head of a mantis.

Lawrence has a light complexion with moles and freck-
les and reddish brown hair that grows out in a thick fuzz.
He comes in the front door with sweat on his face, wearing slippers with high white socks, denim shorts over the
gauze wrapped around his leg, because he got shot in the
thigh a few weeks ago. He flips on the lights with a slow
backhanded lunge, moving into the kitchen, then he turns
on the sink and runs his face under the water, neck craned,
eyes and mouth bobbing open and closed, finally towelling
himself off, his feet planted on the floor at a splayed angle.
He fills a plastic cup with ice, and pours Coke from the two-
liter bottle.

"You used to work at the grocery store," he says to Kendrick. "The Save-A-Lot."

"I worked there for a while, yeah," Kendrick says. "For like a couple weeks I was there."

"The Save-A-Lot," Lawrence says. He looks down into his cup as if mulling over his emotions about this history. "My leg hurts," he says. "I mean, I ain't feeling straight right now, I'm sick, but what I'm trying to say is that we ain't call you because we ain't heard nothing."

From the sofa, Kendrick turns his head to bring Antoinette into his sight as she comes back down the stairs, making a bit of a joke out of how hard he's straining. He's more stoned than he realizes, because now he's scared and trying to figure out why.

"I told him he could stay here and chill out awhile," she says to Lawrence.

"Y'all was students together," Lawrence asks.

"We ain't taking classes now, but yeah, we was students together."

"Students."

There's a blare from both the TV and the stereo as Lawrence navigates his way with two different remote controls. He finally cuts off the TV's sound, then keeps aiming and pushing with his thumb until he cues up the music he wanted.

"Andrea said she waiting for Jodi," he says to Antoinette. "They coming this afternoon, is all she keep saying. Back from Texas. But I just realized that probably means Jodi ain't got her babies with her, if she in Texas. That probably means the babies is next door staying with their daddy. Staying with Damien while she away in Texas or wherever the fuck she is with our money."

He raises his chin at the wall behind the TV. Antoinette looks at him and he shakes his head.

"Jodi has the babies," Antoinette says.

"Maybe."

"You think they next door?"

"I think you better call and find out. I know that I think that."

The music dins and stops, dins and stops. They're talking about Jodi's babies, who are also Damien's babies, because Jodi used to be with Damien who lives next door.

"I'm a get something to eat," says Lawrence.

On the sofa, Kendrick presses his thumb and fingers to the depressions above his eyebrows. He thinks of a fake snapshot of Aysha. He thinks of Lawrence's black Impreza. He thinks of his own face in a mirror, the shadows of his cheekbones. He thinks of himself in his cousin Mason's clothes, his head shaved, sitting there high in Antoinette's living room.

Lawrence comes back with what looks like a hot dog without a bun. He turns up the music and stands there facing the speakers, the room an emptiness that keeps changing size. Kendrick remembers Janelle's trailer, Aysha, Janelle's birthday, the intention of cleaning up the dishes in the sink. Does it mean anything that he intended it, that he intends it even now? He sees dashes of green light, dashes of blue light, dashes of silver light, the music like the undertone of his own pulse, a blooming and unblooming of artificial magnificence. There was a moment as he stood outside the apartment building in the brightness and heat that he noticed the trees behind him—motionless, ghostly—and he realized that he could just turn around and not do this, but the idea of not doing it felt so pure in the moment that it seemed sufficient in itself, so he pushed through it, greeting the boys outside with slow formality in the glare. The craving is like a hunger for air now, a gasping in his veins. It becomes clear all of the sudden that the plans he made before with Antoinette were not about making money but about heroin.

I'll pay-for-it, I'll pay-for-it, I'll pay-for-it, I'll pay-for-it. If I want it, if I want it, if I want it, if I want it . . .

"Andrea, Derrick, Jodi," Lawrence says. "You sitting there listening to everything I been saying just now, like you one of us. Antoinette say you down, all right, I know Antoinette, but I don't know you. I don't know nothing about you."

"I ain't ask you for nothing."

"I thought y'all wanted to get high. So let's go, then, you and me."

Lawrence has a gun tucked into the waistband of his shorts, a small matte black pistol. He has a white towel around his neck that he tugs at rhythmically like a boxer after his warm-up. On the TV, cars chase each other over dark wet roads, street lights passing and going out, passing and going out. Kendrick pictures the ride across town in Lawrence's black Impreza toward some house he can't imagine because he's never done this kind of errand before.

They go outside, Kendrick walking toward the Impreza in the parking lot, but Lawrence moves off to the right, toward the next-door apartment. He thought they were going just the two of them, but now he sees that Lawrence is going to take Damien Martin, too. The boys who were outside are gone now, the office chair sitting empty on the asphalt beside a half-crushed can of iced tea. Damien opens the door. He's older, in his forties, with a black bucket cap on his gaunt head. He has a beard and chipped teeth and he wears a dark T-shirt that says *Kani* in black letters. Behind him, the living room is strung with lights like a bar, red and white bulbs slowly blinking. On a folding table a plastic tray holds the carcass of a rotisserie chicken.

"Jodi got my money," Lawrence says. "We waiting on them all since last night. I ain't hear nothing. I wonder what you heard. If Jodi call you up or something."

Damien looks right at him, his eyes mucus-covered slits.

"They got my money," Lawrence says.

"Jodie over in Metairie," Damien says. "I ain't got nothing for you. I ain't even got no money for you. I got maybe seven, eight dollars."

Lawrence tilts his head like someone patiently communicating with a fool. "I need some help from you, is what I'm saying."

He pulls the gun out of his waistband and points it just to the side of Damien's head.

"Lock the door," he says to Kendrick.

The room seems to recede before them, darker and

darker. Kendrick's throat goes tight, his eyes burning. It
seems obvious from the party lights, the bellowing TV, that
there's nothing here for them to find.

"You ain't hear nothing from Jodi?" Lawrence is saying.
"Nothing from Andrea?"

"I ain't hear from them, man."

"Not one phone call."

"I done told you Jodi in Metairie."

"You told me that. Yeah. Say you got seven, eight dollars. The fuck you think this is?"

Kendrick goes upstairs, because he knows now that
that's why they're here. He sees a rumpled comforter with
green and red stripes, bundles of jackets and pants hanging from hooks screwed into the walls. He sees a picture
on the dresser, Damien and his two girls, white ribbons in
their hair, sitting on their father's knees. He rifles his hands
through the private surfaces of things, lost in a tunnel of
soundlessness. He opens a dresser drawer and finds socks
and underwear and three boxes of different types of cartridges but no gun, no money, nothing.

The noise that comes from the kitchen then is like a
car smashing into an oven. He clamps his hands to his ears,
staggering forward. When he makes it back downstairs, he
sees Damien on his knees, his hands half-raised, his head
pressed between his elbows, his black hat on the linoleum
floor. He has a glaze of red grease on his lips, his mouth
moving in an aftermath of noise. Lawrence shoots him again
with a concussive slam, the gun jerking in his hands, taking
his body with it at a diagonal. Damien twists onto the floor,

hugging himself, while Lawrence shoots him again, the gun coming alive in a different way this time. He looks back at Kendrick as if confused by what he's just done. Blood hangs in a bright ring from Damien's nostrils. One of his ears is slathered red. There's blood on the floor and walls in patterns like ghosts, waterfalls, trees. Kendrick stands there with his ears ringing, a rigidity in his cheeks as if he's grinning against a rush of wind, but in fact his face is blank and his eyes are almost closed.

Lawrence yells something, his body shiny with perspiration, then he sidesteps toward the sliding glass door at the back of the kitchen, head down, skirting the bloodstains on the linoleum, Damien's extended arm. *What you standing there for?* is what he yelled. Damien lies against the dishwasher, his feet up against a plastic bucket, his black T-shirt flapped up to expose his stomach and ribs. The blood in his hair is viscous, dark, but the blood on his skin looks as bright and artificial as dye. Kendrick watches as Lawrence flips the lock and drags the sliding glass door open, creating a sudden rectangle of sunlight and air that he passes through before disappearing.

6

LAGARDE: Okay. Six fifteen. Six thirty. And where did you go then?

KING: I went to Athena Street.

LAGARDE: You went to Athena Street?

KING: Yes.

LAGARDE: You left your girlfriend's and the first place that you went was Athena Street.

KING: Yes.

LAGARDE: And why was that?

KING: I sometimes go to Athena to see friends.

LAGARDE: Friends?

KING: Yes.

A week after the murder, a little after 6:30 p.m. The detective's chair is pushed back far enough that he can cross his legs at the ankles, but it's also close enough that he sometimes leans forward toward Kendrick, his hands braced on his knees, like a coach about to impart some inspiration or advice, though he never does anything but ask more questions. They're in a small room at the back of the sheriff's department, the detective seated catty-corner from Kendrick, not across the table from him, not allowing him the sense of space or protection afforded by the length of even such an insignificant table. He has thinning light hair parted in the middle, brushed back from his forehead, the open face of a boy, but beneath the left eye a half-moon scar like the sear mark left by the edge of a heated bottlecap. It looks still raw, lacquered red against his pale skin. He wears beige slacks, a baby-blue golf shirt—his holstered pistol stands out starkly against this general blandness. His voice is patient, unimpressive, with the kind of New Orleans accent that sounds like Long Island. They've been in the little room for about forty minutes now, the air intimate with the smell of the detective's sport gel deodorant, the metal door closed on the hallway, three of the room's walls covered in white-painted paneling, the fourth, at Kendrick's right shoulder, drywall painted a glossier white. Kendrick resists a current of

sleepiness, barely able to answer for a moment. Everything
he says sounds like a lie now, each clarification just adding
detail to the sense that it's a lie.

Is there any truth to that?

No. No truth at all.

No truth at all.

No, sir.

He sees the smudged black brickwork of the building
on Athena Street, those boys who always linger outside, the
ruined chair that looks pulled out of the trash. Then he sees
the building on the evening of the murder, yellow tape in the
parking lot, the sun still out but the sky starting to darken,
police lights and ambulance lights and Antoinette walking
out in the road toward him like she was drunk. The interview was supposed to be a simple formality—five minutes,
two simple statements: that Kendrick knew who Damien
Martin was, that Kendrick was not present on the morning
of the crime. It was in this spirit that Kendrick had signed
the Miranda waiver, Lagarde softly prompting him, *Okay,
just for the purposes of our investigation, I want to ask you if you would
go ahead and sign this form.*

He sees again the ambulance and the police cars,
Antoinette telling him in the whirling light, *He got shot! He
got shot!*, then the story about cabinets slamming, all she and
Lawrence heard was a sound like cabinets slamming. He tells
this to Lagarde and Lagarde doesn't show suspicion, just asks
about the people at Athena Street, about Kendrick's relationships with Antoinette and Lawrence and even Antoinette's
aunt, Andrea, and now about Damien and Jodi and their

baby. *I wanted to see this little girl, 'cause my little girl is . . . like a few months older. And Jodi said her little girl ain't talking yet. She asked me if it was a problem. Because my lit-tle girl, she . . . she ain't talk till late, like she past two before she really start talking.*

He feels something terrible coming. He knows this because every true thing he says now sounds more and more like a lie.

PART THREE

GAZE

7

"The detective told me he wanted me to be a witness against Jeffries," King testified Wednesday. "I said I didn't know why he wanted me as a witness if I wasn't there.'"

—New Orleans *Times-Picayune*, May 2, 2004

"You will hear that Kendrick King conspired with Lawrence Jeffries and Antoinette Cook to commit an armed robbery for drugs, money, or both, and that this conspiracy led to the murder of Damien Martin. You will hear that the motive for Kendrick King to commit this murder was a need to get high, because he was addicted to drugs, because he was 'sick.'"

—Assistant District Attorney David Campbell, trial transcript, *State of Louisiana v. Kendrick King*

Two versions of a single story. In the first, a black man is saying that a white man's story is fiction. In the second, a white man is saying that a black man's story is fiction. I know which story I would prefer to believe (and I know you know which one you'd prefer to believe), but of course none of that has anything to do with which version is true. It's a problem not just of facts but of imagination. *The crow wished everything was black*, William Blake wrote, *the owl, that everything was white*. He wasn't talking about race. I'm not only talking about race. I'm talking about the problem of seeing anything clearly in the time and place in which we live.

When I was younger, my life in the shadow of my father's death sometimes felt unreal, like a dream before the inevitable waking up that would be my own death. I knew better and yet I didn't—I was also a hedonist, and yet a part of me was drawn to darkness, the infinitude that would affirm my insignificance. My friend Joel once said that the subject of my writing was "the problem of violence." I had thought it was the problem of good and evil, but he was right. I hadn't anticipated that the conversations I had in the rodeo arena at Angola were conversations I'd been waiting to have for most of my life. Almost all the people I spoke to had committed acts of violence. They were intimidating, they looked different from me, they had survived ordeals I would not have survived, and yet I found it easy to talk to them—easier to talk to than strangers with whom I ostensibly had more "in common," even easier to talk to than some people I call friends. There was no elusiveness, no petty negotiations of identity. Eventually, there

was even humor, but it was the kind of humor that grows
not out of trying to outwit each other but out of a playful
testing of commonalities. I valued the humor, but I valued
the commonalities more. It became obvious very quickly
that the conversations were not just about violence but
about injustice. What I mean is that I had to ask myself
why these people had ended up there as prisoners and why
I had ended up there as a journalist (or whatever I was).
Maybe that was the temptation I succumbed to. Maybe I
thought that my identification with people like Kendrick
was a move away from the problem of violence—a move
away from what increasingly felt like an adolescent preoc-
cupation with darkness—toward a more mature concern
for the problem of injustice. Maybe that was why I got so
immersed.

Lawrence Jeffries received a twenty-five-year sentence
for the murder of Damien Martin, the plea deal he'd negotiated in exchange for the information he gave that helped
convict Kendrick. Antoinette Cook also gave information that helped convict Kendrick, and Lawrence, though
all charges against her were eventually dropped. Neither
Antoinette nor Lawrence appeared at Kendrick's trial.
There were no eyewitnesses presented at all. There was no
physical evidence presented connecting Kendrick to the
crime. Kendrick got a life sentence because he wouldn't take
a plea deal, insisting he was innocent and that the police had
coerced a false confession from him.

When I looked again at the *Times-Picayune* article from

May 2, 2004, I saw that of its twenty brief paragraphs, ten were devoted to Kendrick's contention that he was innocent.

> During a series of interviews that August, [Jefferson Parish homicide detective] Lagarde obtained four taped statements from King in which King first denied being in the area but then admitted to accompanying Jeffries into Martin's apartment during the fatal holdup.
>
> But King said that when the recorder was stopped, Lagarde gave him details about the crime to strengthen the case against Jeffries and then instructed King to repeat these details when the recorder was turned on. At one point, King said, Lagarde told him to "fill in the gaps, make it sound more convincing."

The article then reports that Janelle Bryers, Kendrick's girlfriend, had testified that he was at her home when the crime happened. Phone records showed an outgoing call from Janelle's home around the time of the murder. The caller had to be Kendrick, Janelle said, for he was the only one who could have been inside her trailer that day. She was at work. Their daughter, Aysha, was at day care. All this was confirmed by Janelle's coworkers, her time card, and the day care's sign-out book.

Finally, the two witnesses who first identified Kendrick as a person of interest said they saw Kendrick arrive at Athena Street that morning by car, not by bus or on foot, and in Kendrick's second and successive taped statements he says that he drove to the apartment complex in Janelle's car, a Mazda Protégé, because he had no car of his own. But Janelle testified that she had the Mazda Protégé herself that day. She had driven it to work, a fact also confirmed by her coworkers, who in their trial testimony remembered that that day happened to be Janelle's birthday, and they had given her a birthday present, a food dehydrator, which they'd helped her load into the Mazda that evening before she returned home. So while Kendrick could have taken the bus or used some other means to get to Athena Street that day, he could not have taken Janelle's Mazda.

From the trial transcript of *State of Louisiana v. Kendrick King*, May 1, 2004:

10:15   *State closing*
10:40   *Defense closing*
11:02   *State rebuttal closing*
11:25   *Jury charges read*
11:40   *Jury sent to deliberate*
1:12   *Jury reaches guilty verdict*

An hour and a half to reach their conclusions, after a single day of testimony.

You asked if they coerced me, the police, yeah, of course they co-erced me. They had me detained for almost ten hours. There's nothing to eat, no one to talk to, they put you in handcuffs . . . It's not torture, but it's a kind of torture.

I thought of Antoinette Cook, the story of Sonia's

niece in the beauty salon overhearing a woman I now knew was Antoinette declare that there was a man in Angola serving life for a murder he'd had nothing to do with. I said before that there were almost no images online of the people involved in Damien Martin's murder, but when I did some more searching after Deborah and I visited the Old Records Office, I found that Antoinette had started a Facebook page. Her feed showed a heavyset woman in rhinestone-studded sunglasses smoking a joint, or, in another picture, leaning seductively against the door of a car, her mouth pursed in a kiss. There was a photo of her in a Lycra bodysuit, fists planted on her hips, and another of her in a pink sweatshirt drinking a daiquiri out of a large plastic cup. Lawrence Jeffries and Antoinette had had a son at the time of the murder, and there was a photo of the son, now, at fourteen, dressed in a school uniform of khakis and white button-down shirt, looking sternly into the camera, making signs with his hands, Antoinette boasting that she'd got him five school uniforms instead of just one, a clean outfit for every day of the week, hustling for it, getting the money by any means necessary, her son was straight with his school clothes now. I shouldn't have kept looking, but I did. There was a picture of Antoinette and her son visiting what seemed to be Antoinette's sister at the Louisiana Correctional Institute for Women, but the text revealed that the sister was actually Antoinette's aunt, a woman whose name I had no business knowing but did: Andrea, that was her name, Andrea Dufosset, who had once lived on Athena Street, next door to Damien Martin, before Andrea had moved out and left her apartment to Antoinette and her boyfriend Lawrence, in the summer that Damien Martin had been killed.

I thought of Damien's body in a pool of blood beside a bucket of joint compound and a mop in a plastic pail.

He was on his knees, with his hands in the air. Pleading. Begging for his life.

And then the other shots came.

He slumped down after that. I mean, he was out.

I knew now that at his trial Kendrick said that the real reason he had driven to Athena Street on the night of the murder was not to "see friends," but because he wanted to use Antoinette's phone to call an old girlfriend named Desiree Driggs. Desiree Driggs testified in court that he did call her that night. She said he sounded scared. He had just come across a murder scene, he told her. He said he was worried because he'd been at the building earlier that day, and there was a rumor going around that he might have been a lookout during the crime. This at least is what Desiree testified.

I knew I couldn't call Antoinette—she would always have reasons of her own for not talking to someone like me—but I thought Desiree might be able to tell me once and for all what I was getting wrong about this story and then perhaps I could stop thinking about it. She was still in high school when all this happened. When I contacted her, it had been almost a decade since anyone had brought up Kendrick's name, and it was awkward, appearing out of the blue to ask about the ex-boyfriend she'd helped send to prison for life, but she agreed to meet me. On the phone, she confirmed that Kendrick had had some arrests for drugs before the murder. When I asked if Athena Street was a place to pick up heroin, she said she didn't know but that it made sense. Perhaps the reason she was willing to talk to me like this was because she had just spent six years in prison herself. She told me that it had only been two months since she'd been released on parole from St. Gabriel. As we talked, it came out that she knew several of the women I'd met when I went to Angola for the passion play.

We made arrangements to see each other, but when the day came she had car trouble, so we met at a McDonald's she could walk to from where she was living. She was quiet, tall, with long braids knotted behind her head, wearing simple jewelry, jeans, a black sleeveless blouse. I offered to buy her something to eat, but she said she only wanted a Coke, a small Coke, and when the woman at the counter urged her to get a medium, which was the same price as the small, she insisted on the small. Earlier, she had refused my offer to drive her to the McDonald's: no, she'd said, she was fine, she preferred to walk. We sat down at one of the plastic tables and when I asked how she was doing she raised her bowed head, eyes closed, as if to emphasize that she was gathering her thoughts. She was fine, she said, a little tired. It was still strange to be in places like this, ordinary public places like McDonald's.

"I got my driver's license reinstated last week," she said.

"That was something. So I'm trying to find a job now. A couple part time things here and there. Two hundred fifty dollars to get the license back. I'm looking for jobs in places like this, actually—McDonald's."

She smiled facetiously. We'd talked on the phone and exchanged some e-mails, but I didn't know much of her story. She told me that her parole costs were $63 a month and that they continued for fifteen years—it added up to eleven thousand dollars, if she never missed a payment—and she didn't have a job yet. She was staying for now with her sister, her mother helping her a little, and although she was grateful for this, she was also still incredulous about what had happened to her, how her life had gone so differently from what all of them had expected.

"Kendrick, then me, all that in just like three years," she said. "You have to understand, that's not who we were. I was supposed to go to college, the first in my family, that kind of thing."

She showed me a photograph of her and Kendrick from the spring before the murder. He was tall and lanky and wore black shorts and an oversized Houston Astros jersey and he held Desiree close at his side, his other hand reaching up to doff a camouflage bucket hat tilted at an angle on his head. Desiree was dressed in a slate skirt and a white T-shirt with a pink kitten on it, a pink bandanna tied over her hair, matching pink-tinted lenses in her aviator glasses. She gazed into the camera with the deliberate gravity of a pop star. Kendrick smiled faintly, seductively.

"I guess his daughter would have been about two at that point," she said. "And you can see how foolish I am, how happy just to be there."

She told me that they had started dating when she was a teenager. He was three years older, a basketball player, always well dressed, but before long she found out about Janelle, and not long after that, about their baby. Even before his arrest for the murder, she said, she started to give up on what mattered to her: the track team, where she'd won a state championship in the 5,000 meters; her plans for college. She couldn't concentrate on anything but Kendrick. He kept telling her he was going to leave Janelle and come be with her. He was still promising her this the day Damien Martin was killed.

"He was just one of those people," she said. "He wasn't shy, he played everything like it was easy, not serious. He gave me a little purse once, it was from the islands, where his people came from. It was made out of painted wood and it had a face on it. It was like the devil's face, only it was also a sun—the sun with a devil's face. I don't know, he just made you feel like you wanted to know more and more what he was about."

There was a kind of blank period after he went to prison, she went on, in which she somehow failed to get anything done. She had graduated high school by then and was living with her mother, the weeks slipping by, slowly coming to terms with the fact that she wasn't going to the kind of college she'd dreamed of going to—no USC, no out-of-state schools at all, not even LSU—but unable to think beyond this to an alternate plan. She noticed herself and her friends copying traits of characters from movies and TV, their ordinary lives distorted this way into something wittier than they really were. They went to house parties, got drunk, got high—it was a way, she realized now, of not thinking too much about what she'd said at Kendrick's trial, of what it had cost him. It went on like this, and then Katrina happened, and she had to evacuate to Dallas. She moved in with a friend and her friend's uncle. She found a job as a parking attendant at the airport, sitting in the booth at night, living increasingly in her own mind, listening to old CDs on her Discman, while on TV people went to the gym, shopped for groceries, met for drinks, coffee. She moved back to New Orleans eventually, staying with her mother again, this time in a new apartment in Kenner. That was when she began working as an assistant manager at a fast-food restaurant—twenty years old, her mother finally giving her an ultimatum that either she go to community college or join the military.

"And then all of the sudden I just sort of exploded," she told me, looking down at her fingernails. "I was like, why haven't I done any of these basic things? I just needed my own place, my own life. But it was just like when my mother heard about Kendrick. Of course that was the kind of man I'd pick. Of course he had a baby with someone else. Of course he ended up in prison. Because she thought I never took things seriously enough. Because I was spoiled. Because I never saw anything for what it really was."

She asked the young man she was seeing that summer

if he could find a gun, and he said yes, he could, and that
was how they ended up planning the robbery. That whole
night was like a TV show, she said, right up to the moment when they came charging into the BP station and she
saw the woman behind the cash register and it suddenly
became real.

"You just look at this—this lady you never imagined before. She was scared and it was like she thought we weren't
even really human. That's how she looked."

She lost her nerve, shouting out that she was sorry. She
got a ten-year sentence for this. Her boyfriend, who was still
in prison, got thirty years.

She was twenty-eight now, still young, but it was as if
the last seven years had put her at a distance from the world.
She looked bereft, alone with me there in the McDonald's,
wearing a small chain hung with a Chinese symbol. In
the parish jail, she told me—the same place Kendrick had
awaited trial—she had cried all night for weeks, couldn't
eat, could drink only water or milk. She was there for most
of a year, just as he had been. The day her trial was over,
they transported her to St. Gabriel—walking her in handcuffs from the courtroom, to a holding area, then onto the
bus for the two-hour drive. I remembered the women from
St. Gabriel I'd met at Angola, seeing them lined up near
the buses after each rehearsal or performance of the passion play, waiting for their turn to be placed in leg irons
for the ride back. They all wore the same white sneakers,
the same faded jeans, the same blue LCIW shirts—no
makeup, no jewelry, their plain hair pulled back or in a

clip, shapeless and frayed. It was hard for me now to imagine Desiree among them, friends with some of those very
women, but when I asked her about it she told me that she
didn't regret any of her time there. It had made her stronger, more aware. But it was also at St. Gabriel, she said, that
she had her first doubts about the testimony she'd given at
Kendrick's trial. His defense was that he hadn't been there
when the murder happened. He said that under coercion
from the police he'd been made to lie on tape about being there, when in fact he'd been at Janelle's house all that
day. Desiree's testimony contradicted this. What she said
made it easier for the jury to convict him. The person she'd
been in court that day wasn't someone she recognized after
a while, she told me.

"You were eighteen," I said.

"I was young, yes. And I thought I was doing the right
thing, saying what I thought was true. But the thing about
being out of your mind is that you don't know it when it's
happening. You only know afterward. You thought you were
innocent, but you were never innocent. You were full of resentment and anger and pain and all kinds of crazy things."

When she was granted parole two months ago, she
told me, one of the assistant wardens, out of spite, accused
Desiree of "raising her fists" at her. It had been four years
since Desiree had committed any kind of infraction at all
and she would of course have no reason to act out on the
week she was going to be released, but she wasn't surprised,
nor did she allow herself to get angry. Her mother was planning to pick her up that Friday, but the Wednesday before

that Desiree was sent to lockdown without being told why, and once in lockdown she was not allowed to make any phone calls. Her mother drove all the way up from New Orleans, only to be told that her daughter was in a detention cell and would be there for another eight days, then would have to serve an additional thirty days in the general population as further punishment.

"You can't cry in prison," she said. "If you cry, they're gonna put you in a smock"—a green garment with Velcro clasps that you wear in an isolation cell with no sheets on the bed, and no utensils for your meals.

"Like on suicide watch," I said.

"Yes," she said. "Like that."

I asked a difficult question then, the question I most needed to ask.

"Did Kendrick really tell you on the phone that he was at Athena Street the morning of the murder?"

She looked down at her splayed hand on the table and didn't answer.

"I mean, did he say he was there, or did he just say that other people claimed he was there?"

"I don't know," she said. She shook her head in self-reproach. "I started to wonder about that—if I remembered things correctly, if what I said was what really happened."

She was less and less sure as time went by. It had been a confusing year—Kendrick was back and forth with her and Janelle, her and Janelle, and she thought he was finally going to come back with her.

"I mean, that's why he called me that night," she said.

"He was supposed to come over with his things and we were going to move in together. I had a cousin in Slidell, she had an extra room we were going to share. That was where I was when he called that night from the murder scene. In Slidell. At my cousin's. Waiting for him. I mean, that was my state of mind when he made that phone call."

"He stopped at Athena Street on the way to buy drugs," I said.

"Maybe. Either that or he did what they said he did. 'Returned to the scene of the crime.'"

She was on the verge of crying as we stood up to say goodbye. I asked if I could give her a ride back to her sister's apartment, but again she said no, it was fine, she preferred to walk. As we stood there in the nearly empty dining room of the McDonald's, our drink cups still on the table, Desiree putting the photo of herself and Kendrick back into her purse, it occurred to me that her story seemed inevitable but not for any reason. I don't know what that means other than that in the McDonald's her life and mine felt reduced to some essence that had little to do with "identity" or "free will" or even self-interest. What I could discern for now had more to do with pattern, her story growing out of Kendrick's, his trial leading to hers. I thought of the tattoo on Kendrick's arm of the six-pointed star, the Seal of Solomon. I thought of the legend of the biblical king wearing a ring with that symbol on it, signing commands to the good spirits with the brass side, to the evil spirits with the iron side.

*You left your girlfriend's and the first place you went was Athena
Street?*

Yes.

And why was that?

I sometimes go to Athena to see friends.

Friends?

Yes.

8

My own life was going on in its own way. Some friends from out of town came to visit, and Sarah and I took them to dinner at a new restaurant in the neighborhood, partly to celebrate a book I'd just published, a novel set in Israel, New York, and Las Vegas. We walked the three blocks from our apartment to the edge of the French Quarter, the quiet side of the Quarter with its double shotgun houses, slate roofs, gas lamps—the picturesque streets with their wrought-iron balconies and hanging ferns that I went running along most mornings, reminding myself to never take it for granted. Telling people about what I'd seen at Angola never worked very well, though I always tried, because I've never been good at deflecting questions gracefully. After asking, people would make jokes about the food, or they would deliver a solemn comment about the fear of prison as a way of changing the subject. One man, miming this fear, instinctively covered his ass with his hands and made a sheepish face. Our friends from out of town didn't respond like that, they listened to what I had to say, but I couldn't communicate much—I couldn't maintain the sense of calm that would have allowed someone else to understand why I was so interested. They were there to see New Orleans, not to listen to stories about Angola. The sky above us was so richly blue it was more like purple. It was flecked with stars, and the air, scented with jasmine, literally smelled like perfume. Walking in the city on a spring night can feel like walking through a painting (it's too dangerous and dimly lit to feel like walking through a theme park). At the restaurant, we had rice and peas, kale salad, and pork ribs fried in tempura batter—a preposterous dish that our friends agreed to with skepticism, then wanted more of as soon as it was gone. A new friend, Jami, also a writer, met us there. She was about to publish a beautiful novel of her own about a saintly hedonist in Depression-era New York. Another friend, Anderson, had just started working at the restaurant as a bartender, and she sent over a round of free champagne cocktails, in congratulations for my new book. The restaurant had no sign outside. Anyone on the street was free to come in, but few people knew what it was yet, so that night we had it almost to ourselves. Candles burned in little glasses on the bar. The room had black wooden beams on the ceiling, the plaster on the walls worn away to reveal the brick beneath, and it felt, as it was meant to, like some tavern in a mythical Caribbean from two hundred years ago. I knew that even one night like this was the sign of a rich life. I had nights like this all the time. A toast to my new book, a toast to Jami's—as I said, my life went on as I looked deeper and deeper into Kendrick's.

9

About eight months after I'd first met Kendrick, the prison
put on another performance of the passion play, though
it was still half a year from Easter, which would have
been a more fitting time. On our first morning back that
November, Deborah and I had breakfast at what was called
the ranch house along with a half dozen assistant wardens
and a sound crew from Texas, all of us seated at a long table
in office chairs whose casters rolled awkwardly when we
moved toward or away from our food, the walls before us
hung with framed memorabilia from the prison rodeo. An
inmate cook with a bald head and huge hands, dressed in
kitchen whites, asked if anyone wanted more to eat, while
his inmate helper circulated the table with coffee and orange juice. It cost $1.50 a day to feed a prisoner in Louisiana,
fifty cents a meal. Wages for inmates working in the fields
at Angola started at nothing for the first three years, then
went up to two cents an hour, then gradually rose to twenty
cents but no higher. We had eggs, bacon, grits, biscuits, jam

made from brown turkey figs grown specially for the warden on the prison grounds. I looked at my notebook from our first visit. *I like W, he's angry. Says he's not going to make any more mistakes. Learned his lesson. Going to get out and be a cook. Later, he tells me his father is also here, also serving life.* After breakfast, the cook showed me a stuffed alligator head the warden kept in his office, along with a painting of a Native American woman on black velvet that hung above his desk. I had told Deborah before that I felt less comfortable at the ranch house with the administrators than in the prison itself with the inmates. After breakfast, she and I drove through the fields toward the rodeo arena, and she said, "I think I'm lost," and we both laughed as if it were some double entendre, though she wasn't really joking.

The arena was as always forbidding, dreamlike, a dusty oval where people gathered in groups, talking in a way they only did among themselves, a way that changed the moment someone like me came close. From a distance, I saw Kendrick with some other men lined up for a count, none of them in costume yet but still in street clothes—baseball caps and silkscreened T-shirts, some of them wearing basketball shoes and wristwatches and even gold chains, the shoes so clean they glowed. Two corrections officers, a woman and a man, were shouting out unit designations—ASH TWO, ASH FOUR—and small groups of inmates belonging to each unit slowly shuffled their way down the grandstand to stand in front of the guards military-style, responding to their names when they were called out one by one. Kendrick wore jeans, a white baseball cap with a folded bill, a black

T-shirt with an image on it of a rustic cross and the words THIS CHANGES EVERYTHING in white letters. I'd forgotten how big he was, how he and so many of the others had the bodies of boxers or football players. He'd been sulking the last time I'd seen him in something other than a costume, and the time before that he'd been struggling not to cry. He was the last in his unit this morning to be called. He walked up in a lazy slouch and gave a look of fixed contempt to the guard in his sunglasses. The guard ordered him to stand closer. They looked at each other for what seemed a long time, then Kendrick grudgingly shifted his feet forward less than an inch. The guard yelled, "Thank you," which of course meant the opposite. Then Kendrick walked back up the grandstand, avoiding people's eyes, still not seeing me. Eventually, I walked up behind him and put my hand on his shoulder and said his name, which caused him to turn.

"What you got?" he said.

He breathed in slowly through his nose, taking me in, not recognizing me at first. When he finally did, I sensed his resentment over how long I'd been out of touch. I explained that the administration had not allowed me to write to him, that if I'd written more than the little thank-you cards I'd sent, I would not have been allowed to be here now. We were standing in the dirt, surrounded by fences, a sign behind Kendrick's head saying DANGER WILD CATTLE, and I realized how uncomfortable I was with knowing how much I now knew about him, how much had changed since he'd first told me his story. I asked if his mother had said hello for me and he said yes.

"People been messing with me this morning," he said. "Just one of those days. If my mind seems off, that's why."

I asked him what had just happened with the guard and he quoted something he said he'd read in Leonardo da Vinci: *There are three classes of people. Those who see. Those who see when they are shown. Those who do not see.*

"I never heard that," I said.

"He said that like five hundred years ago. Leonardo."

We kept walking. I thought of how many ways I always found to waste my time, and how I often resolved to stop living that way, and how I never did.

"When you talked to my mother, she told you about my brother, Marcus?" he asked.

"A little."

"He's staying with her now—she's sick, she needs help. I ain't seen Marcus in like eleven years, but now he's down here to take care of our mother. What I told you about the guards—it's not the guards. I don't belong in here. My mother's going to be leaving soon. She ain't say nothing, but she's sick, and Marcus has a life in New York. He has a job. He ain't going to stay down here, he's going bring her up there."

"You don't know that."

"Those who see. Those who see then they are shown. Those who do not see."

He was leading us into the chute below the grandstand where the others were waiting in line to get their costumes. I felt their eyes on us, and the eyes of the guards, and I remembered this feeling from before: my self-consciousness about discussing his life in front of other people, his complete lack of self-consciousness about it. I felt foolish listening again to his story as he told it to me all over again, knowing so much more about it now than he realized, knowing also that he wasn't telling me everything. He insisted again that he was innocent—didn't I see that? He didn't say he was a bystander or a lookout, or that he was only involved because he was sick and needed drugs. He just said he wasn't there. But when I asked him, he still had no good explanation for why he would have driven to Athena Street that Monday evening after the murder. He told me that the main thing he was worried about that night was leaving Janelle. He felt bad about it, but he also felt trapped, and the only other place he had to go besides his mother's was Desiree's. He didn't want to make a "blank trip," he said—he didn't want to drive all the way to Desiree's new place in Slidell if she wasn't there, so he stopped at Athena Street on the way to call her. He said that it had nothing to do with drugs, that he'd stopped using drugs by then. If he was a heroin addict, he said, he would have gone into withdrawal during his interrogation, which was only a week after the murder. "I would have been sick out my mind," he said, reminding me that the interrogation lasted almost ten hours. I listened to all these things he said and thought he was lying, then telling the truth, then lying, all the while trying to listen to new information he was presenting, some of which I missed because I was trying to assess the veracity of it all. The tunnel we were in seemed to get narrower and narrower, leading us back toward a little alcove built into the brown-painted gates where the inmate who designed the costumes was working on the makeup of the inmate who played Jesus. The actor had his shirt off in the cold, studying his script in front of a space heater the size of a toaster oven, its wires lit up orange, while the other man applied strips of paper towel and latex to his naked back. From a distance, it would appear as a vividly gory mess of red, yellow, and gray—Jesus' lash marks. I was being approached now by other inmates I knew from my previous visit. Gumarus, Solomon, Quntos, Pamela, Wilbert, Cherie, Troy, Terrence, Layla, Khristian, Zeno—all of these people and more, the men walking up to me, the women looking at me from farther off, and I nodded and put a hand on Kendrick's shoulder, an awkward gesture because I was holding a notebook and pen, and told him we could talk more later. My father was the victim of a persuasive liar, I thought. My father was murdered for what he came to know about another person's secrets. It would make sense for me to be a suspicious person, though in fact I was less, not more, prone to suspicion than most people. If his mother left New Orleans, he would have no one to visit him. Most inmates here never had visitors. Suspicious of what, I asked myself. If he was telling the truth, then it was a sad story. If he was lying, then it was just sad in a different way.

The flogging of Christ took place behind a plastic wall that had been spray-painted to give the illusion of piled stones, a screen hiding from view the source of the loud whip cracks coming over the PA system. When the actor who played Jesus finally came out into the open, a woman seated in front of me in the grandstand actually averted her eyes. His wounds appeared that graphic, even from all the way across the arena—blood, viscera, torn skin. Behind him in a classically composed tableau of utter calm stood ranks of Roman soldiers in red, the consul's red throne, the red banners of the Roman tribunal. "Behold the man," Pilate said. "The sight of his battered and bleeding body will surely satisfy your craving for revenge. Watch and see if you are not shaken by it." But the crowd was not shaken. Instead, they shouted, "Crucify him! Crucify him!" and so they brought out the cross. Christ in His crown of thorns walked through the arena like a figure in some sadistic carnival, awkwardly shouldering the instrument of His death, stumbling, falling, helped back to His feet, while the mob kept jeering, throwing stones, eager to kill Him themselves. On the dirt mound behind Him, the two thieves were already hanging from their crosses. A soldier announced, "You will be taken to the Place of the Skull, where as an example to others, you shall be nailed to the cross until you are dead." They forced Him to the ground, then tied His arms to a wooden beam. They nailed His hands and He screamed, then they hauled the cross upright on ropes and nailed His feet and He screamed again. He hung there in agony, crying out to the god who had forsaken Him, asking why, but of course there was no why and there was no reprieve. Someone tried to assuage His thirst by giving Him some sour wine on a sponge attached to a stick. *As an example to others, you shall be nailed to the cross until you are dead.*

When the play was over, we talked again at the lunch tables, Kendrick back in his ordinary clothes. There were quartered sandwiches of ham, turkey and cheese, tuna salad on white bread, along with Doritos and cookies. Kendrick sat next to me with twelve sandwiches laid out neatly on his plate, all the same kind, nothing else. I remembered the night before when Deborah and I had arrived to find the main prison already dark, the dormitory quiet as we climbed the stairs, each riser printed with red letters on a yellow ground saying WATCH YOUR STEP, and WATCH YOUR STEP printed on each wall of each landing.

"You never heard that from Leonardo?" he asked.

"No."

"You think I'm ignorant, I understand that, but I'm trying, getting there. Baby steps."

He told me he'd read the notebooks of Leonardo after reading Machiavelli's *The Prince*. Machiavelli, Sun Tzu—they were popular in Angola. Somehow Leonardo's notebooks had led him to architecture—Frank Lloyd Wright, Mies van der Rohe, Le Corbusier—form following function, the golden ratio—and he suddenly started noticing buildings for the first time, he said, the way the spaces people constructed were a reflection of what they believed. He actually said "we," not "people," as if he still played a part in this exchange and had not been exiled from the world of people and what they believed. He asked me again to write to him and I told him again that I couldn't do that. He said there were ways. I asked him once again the question about why he had gone to Athena Street on the night of the murder, knowing the answer would just be the nonanswer about not wanting to drive all the way to Slidell on a "blank trip," and he repeated this story and wouldn't clarify. The more I pressed, the more he resisted.

I happened to have gone to a show at the Guggenheim Museum a few months before this, an installation by the artist James Turrell, who had set up colored lights that turned slowly from green to blue to purple to pink inside the museum's spiraling rotunda. I had a picture of it on my phone and I showed it to Kendrick, explaining what it was, that the building was designed by Frank Lloyd Wright, that the pink lights were revealing the inside of it—those halos of light were the concentric rings of the museum's rising levels. He looked at it—the cell phone, the image, the architecture, the installation—the totality of those things. He kept the phone in his hand, though now he looked off in the distance toward the arena. He said he had to process it for a minute. He said he had more thoughts than he could get out right then. I somehow knew that one of those thoughts was an understanding that I no longer believed him. A part of me thought that he'd been there in that kitchen during the murder and I knew that he sensed it.

"You should talk to my brother, Marcus," he finally said. "Just call my mother, she'll put him on. He's an architect, actually. Even before I got here, he stopped talking to me.

The burning barn, remember that? Ha. Imagine you're trapped in
a burning barn? Not because of something you did, but for
no reason. Because it's just like that for you."

"But not for Marcus."

"He has his problems too, I'm sure. Very different problems. I could only guess." He shook his head, smirking a little. "Look at where we are."

We were outside the arena under a plastic tent eating
quartered sandwiches on trays. *The burning barn, remember
that? Ha.* I remembered a passage I'd written about my first
visit here with Deborah. On our last day, we had packed
up her truck and were pulling out of the parking area to
leave for home, when our path was blocked by an old inmate awkwardly pushing an overloaded cart full of props
and other odds and ends. He looked like something out of
Hieronymus Bosch—long white hair, an unkempt white
beard, his body stooped over and wizened. Whenever I'd
seen him that week, he would be cleaning up trash or running errands at the edge of panic, a servile figure with such a
skittish manner that almost everyone avoided even looking
at him. We waited for him to move, then he waited for us to
move, then finally we drove past him. He had once been a
U.S. Marine, Deborah told me—he'd been decorated for his
service in the Middle East. In Deborah's old photograph of
him from 1999, which she showed me when we got home, he
was unrecognizable. He was dressed for the rodeo—prison-
striped shirt, cowboy hat, short black hair, a well-groomed
mustache. His event back then was "Guts or Glory." In
"Guts or Glory," you vie with a group of other inmates to

pluck a poker chip from between the horns of a charging bull. Deborah told me these things about him as we drove away from the prison, and I thought about him now as I sat at that picnic table next to Kendrick, knowing how unlikely it was that either man would ever leave that place.

10

I called Sonia after a few days to say I'd seen Kendrick, and though I didn't speak to Marcus, it was through Sonia that I ended up meeting Janelle Bryers a few months later. Sonia called again to tell me that Janelle had contacted her after receiving in the mail a photograph of Kendrick taken by Deborah at Angola. Deborah sent thousands of these prints to inmates so they could keep them as mementos or share them with loved ones—several inmates had reconnected in this way with family members who had long since fallen out of touch. It turned out that Kendrick's daughter, Aysha, now thirteen, had started writing to him shortly before this. That was how he learned of her and Janelle's address in Houston, which was how he knew where to send Aysha his portrait.

"So maybe now I'll see her someday," Sonia told me. "Houston's not that far away."

She was cheerful by nature, which always made me feel somewhat intrusive when I contacted her. When I asked

her about her health, she said she was "doing fine," then as-
sured me that she was not planning to leave New Orleans
anytime soon. She said she had already discussed this with
Marcus—he was paying for someone to help her get to and
from her dialysis treatments when he couldn't be there.

"It's not so bad," she said. "It's not as bad as I thought.
If I give it a few more times, I know it will get easier. In
the meantime, they put me in a commercial. SureFire. You
know that?"

"No."

"Oh, SureFire. I'm going to send you the information."

She sent me a text with a link to a video of her in her lab
coat talking about how SureFire, a staffing company, had
found her her job. After this brief testimonial, she laughed
at herself a little, then clapped her hands and recited the
company's jingle.

I called Janelle later that day. I told her I'd gotten her
number from Sonia and that I'd been talking to Kendrick,
but she stopped me, saying she knew who I was.

"I've been meaning to call you," she said. "Sonia gave me
your number. I read your book, or I read most of it. I didn't
finish it. I couldn't, really."

Before she could elaborate, she had to go—she was at
work, she said. We had a number of interrupted conversations like this. She was a nurse at an assisted-living facility
and she was also starting a catering business with a friend
who owned a restaurant. If the catering business took off
like her friend's restaurant—it was confusing, the friend actually owned two restaurants, it turned out—then Janelle

could give up nursing, which she'd wanted to do for a long time. She was overworked, and I couldn't tell from her tone how she felt about talking to me, but part of the problem was that I myself didn't really know why I was talking to her. We kept getting interrupted by her many obligations, so we would make plans to talk again later, simply because we'd been interrupted, and in this way, out of some misunderstanding, I began to seem more purposeful than I was. In part, she wanted to talk to me about her daughter, Aysha. I think it was the seriousness of Kendrick's predicament that made her want to talk to me about this. I'd written a book she couldn't finish because it was too upsetting. I'd had some experience with the unacceptable. It was a strange book—a "conjuration," I'd called it, an attempt to bring my father back to life in a way I could actually feel. You had to watch it unfold for a while before you could trust what I was doing, making characters where there had only been names and facts, imagining the people as though they were real and not ciphers. That Janelle had trusted it enough to find it upsetting meant something to me. We had something to talk about, I thought, though we never had time to talk about it. Eventually, I told her I had friends in Houston. I wanted to talk to her in person, too, though I wasn't sure why.

I drove to Houston, which, as Sonia had said, is not that far from New Orleans. I arrived a little late to our appointment at Janelle's friend's restaurant on Richmond Avenue. I thought at first that I was at the wrong place because neither Janelle nor her friend were around. A young waiter in a black shirt and black tie came to greet me at the hostess stand and told me to wait there while he looked for the owner. The restaurant looked brand new, with red banquettes and black lacquered tables on gleaming white floors. The huge dining room and bar were completely empty, R. Kelly's "I Believe I Can Fly" playing over the speakers to no one. The owner would be out in a minute, the waiter told me. I sat at the bar and ordered a drink and looked at my phone. I kept seeing a woman every now and then returning from the kitchen to talk to a man who was fixing the restaurant's point-of-sale system, and this woman turned out to be the owner. Janelle, she explained, was running some errands but she'd be there soon. Eventually, Janelle herself called me.

"I'm sorry," she said. "My son has an ear infection. We been at the doctor's office, back and forth, twice this week. I'm just all over the place right now."

I didn't know she had a son. I asked if he was all right.

"We can talk some other time, if that's better," I said.

"No, there is no better. Can we do it at my house maybe? In like an hour or two?"

"Your house?"

"We can do it there and I can get them something to eat. Once I get my son to bed, it will be easier. I'm sorry for this, I just need to get him taken care of."

I sat there after we hung up and ordered dinner, in order to allow them time to get settled. I had a catfish sandwich, which came on too dense a roll and was greasier than it would have been in New Orleans, which made me feel farther from home. Eating in that still-empty restaurant I felt the kind of vacancy you feel when there's no one around

to prove to you that you're real. I paid my check and thanked
the owner and went out to the parking lot with its painted
lines and arc lights. It was dark now. I sat in the car and
pulled up Janelle's address on my phone and drove there
with no music on.

We sat at a dining table outside Janelle's kitchen, the room
dimly lit by a single lamp, her son, Andre, in bed now, her
daughter, Aysha, gone to do her homework in Janelle's room
but her plate still there, still bearing a few bits of fish sticks
and macaroni and cheese. I'd sat there while Aysha ate
her dinner, noticing how much she looked like Kendrick,
though her eyes were dark brown, not caramel-colored. She
was still wearing her school uniform, red plaid with a white
shirt with a Peter Pan collar, a little cluster of white beads
braided into one strand of her shoulder-length hair. I told
her who I was and that I'd met her father, that I'd talked to
him several times, and like her mother she told me that she
knew that already. I said I was glad she was writing letters
to him.

"It's not letters," she said. "It's e-mail. Prison e-mail.
You have to pay for it every time, it's not free."

I thought of that tone now, which reminded me of
Kendrick, as Janelle poured herself a glass of red wine, saying she hoped I didn't mind. She offered me some, then said
that the wine was typical of Houston, which was "bougie."
There was no culture, not like in New Orleans, but the job
market, the cost of living—you could get a two-bedroom

apartment like this for $800 a month. Andre's toys were
all over the floor and on the table, but the room had large
windows, the building was brand new, the furniture new. It
had seemed like an obvious step up, she told me, until she'd
started to have problems with Aysha last year, an adolescent
now, and Janelle faced that with no extended family in town
to help her. She said there was a "spark" Kendrick always
had that he'd passed on to their daughter, a curiosity they
shared—if you pointed to a country on a globe, Aysha would
name it, sometimes even tell you its capital—but she'd
started to conceal this side of herself, just as Kendrick had
sometimes done. My aloneness at the restaurant earlier was,
I saw now, a premonition of what it would be like here now,
in this room. She was talking about Aysha's resemblance to
Kendrick, the genetic connection between them, and it reminded me of a home movie I'd seen of my father, a tiny
three- or four-second snippet of him in which he's shown
moving a garden hose at the side of our house in Phoenix
not long before he was killed. It's a mystery as to why such
an insignificant moment was filmed at all, and yet because
of the way he moves his body (he would have been in his late
thirties) it was like watching a clip of myself doing the same
task, half-attentively, partly there and partly somewhere
else.

Aysha, she said now, had gotten into trouble at school
last month—she'd been accused of stealing a classmate's
cell phone. What had actually happened was that the other
girl had been taunting Aysha for days, and in retaliation
Aysha had thrown the girl's phone, cracking its screen on

the asphalt of the playground. The girls fought. When they were finally separated, the other girl was taken to the nurse's office. Aysha was arrested—she was put in handcuffs and forced into the back of a police car. It upset her so much that she wouldn't talk for two days. She went blank, rather than crying, which was worse, Janelle said. She told me she knew the arresting officer because his aging father was one of her patients at the assisted-care facility.

"He said he was sorry, the officer," she said.

I looked at her.

"Yeah," she said. "He said he didn't know she was my daughter. He was very sorry for that."

She was still wearing her blue scrubs from work. She steepled her hands over her nose in a way that alarmed me at first until I realized that she wasn't about to cry but was only thinking.

"He didn't kill anyone," she said.

"Who?"

"When I came home that night from work, he had been there in that trailer all day, it was obvious. Kendrick had that certain look he got. He was sitting on the couch and I could see how he was. He had cleaned up the dishes—he was trying to be nice to me because it was my birthday—I mean, it wasn't like he cleaned up in some crazy way, frantic or something. He just cleaned up the house a little. But he was tired of being in there, you could see that. It was just a little trailer house and he'd been there all day."

I knew more about the evening she was talking about than I wanted to. I knew for example that her coworkers had given her a food dehydrator that afternoon as a birthday present. I wondered if Kendrick had helped her carry it out of the car and into the house that evening before he left to go to Athena Street; if she'd looked at the food dehydrator after he was gone and if it had made her feel more alone.

She told me he seemed stoned when she came home from work, but she didn't want to fight, though they fought a little anyway—that was how it was with them, not talking and then finding a way to fight anyway. He took the car and went somewhere. She and Aysha were both asleep by the time he came back. Perhaps she sensed he was sitting up awake in the other room—sometimes she just woke up in the middle of the night for no reason—in any case she found him alone in the dark, the TV on but the sound off, his face gray in the flickering light. He was listening to his Discman, staring at the changing patterns on the screen, not moving even when she touched his arm. She'd been angry with him for leaving her on her birthday, but she knew now that something more serious was happening. When he stopped the music, he was deliberate, quiet, cold—he'd been taking care of some business, he said. Then he told her matter-of-factly that he was moving out tomorrow. It wasn't tearful—she was annoyed and he was sullen. She pressed him to say what was really wrong, why he was upset, and he finally told her that someone he knew had been shot that morning, someone at the place he'd just been. She asked him if he was okay and he said he didn't know. He didn't know how he was just then.

"When I see her stand a certain way," she said then.

"When I'm behind her, or when I catch her out of the corner of my eye, she'll be standing in a certain way that looks just like him. Sometimes it makes me smile and sometimes it makes me want to slap her. Or even talking like he did. She couldn't *know* he talked like that. Almost the same words he would use."

I told her then about the home movie of my father, how strange it was to see myself reflected in those images of him beside our house, how I had watched the little clip over and over, amazed by how young and ordinary he was. I talked about writing my book about him, how I had thought it would make me a different person, stronger and more at ease in the world, and how I did become that kind of person for a brief time but that it didn't last, or rather that it came and went in unpredictable ways.

Aysha was still in her school uniform, the white shirt untucked so that its tails hung over the plaid skirt in a way that foregrounded the absurd gentility of the whole outfit. She had come back out from Janelle's bedroom, no doubt aware that we'd been talking about her and her father. What struck me was how Janelle's face turned softer, almost solicitous, for just a second before it went hard again.

"You been eavesdropping," she said.

"No."

"What time is it?"

"I don't know. Nine."

"So do the math on that. When is bedtime?"

"I can't do the homework. Like I said, I tried. I don't understand what they're asking."

Like her father, she was self-possessed to the point of intransigence, standing there with her arms at her sides in such a way that the uniform now seemed to have nothing to do with her at all. Eventually, I tried to help her with her homework, following her back into Janelle's bedroom while Janelle started cleaning up in the kitchen. I stood there in that private space, my hand on the dressing table, as Aysha grudgingly showed me what she was working on.

It was a poem by Dorothy Parker called "Solace," in which the speaker, perhaps a girl about Aysha's age, recounts the indifference of the people around her to life's sadness. A rose fades, a bird dies, a lover disappears—these are the trite examples of the girl's encounters with loss and insignificance.

Annotate for diction only, the instructions below the poem read, followed by the questions:

    1. *What is the tone of the poem?*

    2. *What is the theme of the poem?*

I didn't know a lot about Dorothy Parker, but I knew she was famous for her cutting wit, and yet "Solace" was the example of her work they'd unearthed, the specimen of "poetry" they'd seen fit to offer to Aysha and her classmates. She was right to resist such an assignment, but she had to do it anyway.

I asked her what she thought the poem meant. What did it have to say, for example, about the dead rose, the dead bird, the lover who had fled? What did all those things have in common? She asked me what the word *solace* meant and I told her. The more we looked at the poem the more complicated it became, the more there was to see, even in such a thin piece of work.

"Like praying?" she said about the word *solace*.

"Sometimes," I said.

"Telling people it's going to be all right."

> *There was a bird, brought down to die;*
> *They said, "A hundred fill the sky—"*

Her face went still as she went through some progression of understanding, then foreboding. This is what the world requires of us, to take whatever she was feeling in that moment and state it in simple terms.

The tone of the poem is sad.

The theme of the poem is that no one will offer you solace.

11

LAGARDE: Are you okay?

KING: What?

LAGARDE: You seem like you might be nauseated or something.

KING: No. I'm all right. I had just belched.

The door opens and another detective comes in wearing black pants and a white polo shirt with the dark blue insignia of the homicide section on it. Kendrick watches as he and Lagarde have a brief conversation about someone else's case, their sudden indifference to him worse than their attention. About an hour has passed since they finished recording the first tape. The other detective holds several manila folders bundled inside a larger one, all of them rumpled with reuse, the papers inside disheveled. When he and Lagarde finish talking, he leaves the folders with Lagarde, then closes the door behind him, and Lagarde sits back down, this time across the table from Kendrick, looking over the new information. They sit there in silence for a while. On the table is what Lagarde had called the "six-pack," a grouping of six close-up photos of young black men, all but one of them in a white T-shirt, their faces scared, defiant, incredulous—it's impossible to know what any of them were feeling when the pictures were taken. The face of Lawrence Jeffries seems more inquisitive than the others, his gaze meeting the photographer's gaze as if asking him how it feels to do such a job. There's a spot on Lawrence's white T-shirt just below the collar, too dark to be a bloodstain, almost black, and Kendrick wonders what it is, wonders how long they've had Lawrence in custody, what he's been saying. Everything so far has been quiet, secretive, Lagarde never raising his voice or growing accusatory, but after a while it becomes hard to remember what they know and what they've just imagined about him, what he knows about himself and what he's just imagined. The longer he sits there, the more he begins to imagine himself as a twenty-one-year-old black male like all the other twenty-one-year-old black males, divorced from his life like the young men in the photographs are divorced from theirs. Lagarde goes to the door again and summons the other detective, holding his hand out behind him as if to signal to Kendrick that it will just be a few more seconds. When he sits back down, he wipes the sides of his nose with the first two fingers of both hands.

"So, you know, the tape's not running right now," he says. "But let's just clarify a few things before you make the ID, then you can leave, all right? Just five or ten more minutes."

In the manila folder is a 9-by-12 envelope that turns out to contain a series of color photographs. At the top of the stack is a picture of Damien Martin. He's lying dead on the linoleum floor, his black T-shirt twisted back from his torso, blood spreading out and pooling beside the yellow dishwasher. Kendrick sees it before he even looks at it. He feels a surge of panic and guilt that is the feeling of being in jail. Then he gradually understands that the only alternative to being in jail right now is to stay in this room with Lagarde, looking at the photographs.

12

A Monday in August, 2003. He stands in front of the black-out curtain and faces the room making signs with his hands, moving in rhythm to a song he isn't quite hearing, higher than he wants to be, the blunt still burning, more than half of it left. It's a little after four, the kitchen cleaned up, dishes in the rack, all the cups and brightly colored bowls stacked in their jumble. Outside it's too hot to stand even in the shade, no one visible for the last couple hours, the trailer houses withering like ruins beneath the trees. He sits on the sofa and presses his thumb and fingers to the depressions above his eyebrows, letting his right index move up to feel the scab. Five days drifting after ten days in jail, everything getting tangled up, converging, so that just as he'd promised to move in with Desiree he'd run into Antoinette, his mind turning stupidly, in spite of himself. On Friday, he shaved his head to rid himself of this feeling, but it's still there, the stench of bodies in jail—no phone call, no lawyer, no way of even knowing how much time was passing. He tried to squat against the wall in the holding cell, the lights going out and a dimmer set coming on orange, while they threw in some sandwiches wrapped in plastic. When he closes his eyes now, he sees dashes of green light, dashes of blue light, dashes of silver light, the music in his head like ice on a green lake.

He's still sitting there two hours later when Aysha comes running in through the door, happily screaming, the screen slamming, Janelle behind it, not having seen him yet. There's that glazed quality that things take on in bright sunlight when you have something caught in your eye. The people at work had given her a birthday present, she tells him. They go out and get the gift from the car, a food dehydrator in a large box with bright pictures on the sides of apple slices, strawberries, kiwi, pineapple. By the time he puts the box on the kitchen counter it's as though they've been having an argument the whole time, though they haven't been speaking at all.

"It's hot out there," she says, once they're back inside.

"Yeah, hot," he says. He sits back on the couch, Aysha already crawling onto his lap, Kendrick waving a lazy hand at her to stop. "You have a nice day?"

Janelle's still looking at the gift in its box. Drops of perspiration glisten at the back of her neck where her hair begins, fastened in a bun above the collar of her belted sweater, which she wears because the air-conditioning at work is too strong.

"I don't know what it's supposed to mean," she says. "It's like it's some kind of statement or something. Like I need to eat more healthy."

"You mean like some kind of moral statement."

She picks up Aysha and holds her on her hip, Aysha's head on her shoulder, not paying attention to him anymore. "You see this?" she says to Aysha. "Look at what those ladies at work got for us."

"I need to use the car for a minute," he says.

"Huh?"

"I'm sorry—I just got to do something quick. Serious. Like less than an hour. It's not a moral statement. It's just like a transportation statement."

"Yeah, keep joking."

She turns and looks at him, then she holds Aysha closer and kisses her check so she doesn't have to see him anymore. He thinks of the moment at the mall yesterday when she told him to wipe Aysha's face, *Clean up her face, Kendrick*, and he took the wipe and bent down over Aysha in the stroller and saw her cheeks, her nose, so intricate and small she seemed to have been shaped from a mold. *Clean up her face, Kendrick*: it was not just bossing, it was a sign that he was welcome again, that she felt comfortable enough to play it like everything was normal.

"Hey," he says.

"I really don't got anything for you right now," she says, turning and looking at the refrigerator. "You do what you want."

The car is still cool from her drive home across the river. His clothes are damp in places from just those few moments

outside and now the damp spots begin to get cold from the
AC. There's no one outside to see him gripping the steering wheel with both hands as he moves around the slow
U of the trailer park—breezeways of aluminum and wood,
chain-link fence, plastic furniture, toys. He stops at the
stop sign and stares ahead and doesn't start moving again
for a long time. *Clean up her face, Kendrick.* It had been good,
his baby girl, he couldn't believe how it made him feel, but
then all this drifting, the day wasted, sitting in the trailer
waiting for someone to call or come by.

On Ames Boulevard, there's a gas station and an old sign
for a Sno-ee stand with almost all its letters missing, NOM
OPEZ instead of NOW OPEN, not open, nothing there. He
drives through a semirural landscape that he doesn't see—
an Exxon station, culverts, power lines, houses of dark brick.
The highway becomes a long bypass overlooking denser
neighborhoods clotted with fast-food restaurants and auto-
parts dealers. To his left is the older city on the other side of
the river—the French Quarter, the Superdome—all those
places he hardly ever sees, but that was where they arrested
him fifteen days ago for no cause, his face pressed against
the asphalt on Ursulines Avenue, a cellophane wrapper
from a pack of cigarettes a few inches from his face, which
he had no choice but to look at when he opened his eyes.
Stop spitting, you're spitting on yourself, the cop said, pushing him
into the back of the car, the cut above his eye swelling into
a tight ball, the handcuffs inducing a kind of panic that almost took his breath away.

He keeps watching himself extend the mistake of leaving

her on her birthday and even regrets making it, while another part of him pretends that it can't be important. He takes a fork off the Terry Parkway just past the Oakwood mall and heads toward Athena Street, the sun still out but the sky starting to darken a little, so that the clouds look monumental against the turquoise swell. There's no breeze, only heat, the trees motionless, their leaves a chaos of shining green, gold, black shadow, some covered entirely in thick vines. It's the hour before people start coming out of their apartments to finally take in the air, the aimless hissing of cicadas, the fish smell of garbage, a few kids out on their bikes, traffic clunking by. One of the vine-shrouded trees is like a hooded figure pointing at the apartment complex across the road from it. He sees the police lights in the corner of his right eye—at least three cars and an ambulance, yellow tape in the parking lot and a loose group of maybe a dozen people lingering there. His heart dips and clenches. Instinctively, he just keeps driving, neither speeding up nor slowing down. He takes a right a few intersections later, realizing that he needs to find out what's happening, then backtracks around to the rear of the apartment complex. The complex consists of several identical structures over the space of several blocks, and he parks across the street from Antoinette's unit, finding an unobtrusive spot near a fenced-in Dumpster, a gaping hole in the brickwork of the exterior wall that he stares at for a moment before he turns his gaze to the rearview mirror and sees the police lights and the ambulance lights and even a corner of the yellow tape. He sees Antoinette then, walking out in the road toward his car. He gets out and tries to steer her back toward the group of onlookers, Antoinette moving like she's drunk, telling him in the whirling light, *He got shot! He got shot!*, everything getting tangled now, the sky pulsing in its blueness, bluer than it's been all day. *He got shot! He got shot!* He walks through the police tape, because he isn't thinking— he wants to move away from Antoinette and he just walks through it. It turns out that Lawrence is watching in the distance, denim shorts over the gauze wrapped around his leg where he was shot a few weeks before. *They saw your car,* he tells Kendrick later, when they're all inside Antoinette's apartment. *What car?* Kendrick says. *The car you drove here in this morning,* Lawrence says.

13

Another six months passed—it had been more than a year now since I first met Kendrick. That May, a Christian nonprofit organization came to Angola to put on an event called "Returning Hearts," which reunited inmates with their children. The prison expected 951 kids to arrive that morning. Waiting there for them were 371 inmates, along with 700 Christian volunteers to serve as chaperones, for the children would be there all day, a long time for families who in many cases hadn't seen each other in many years, if ever. It had been ten years since Kendrick had seen Aysha. I was hoping she would come but I hadn't heard back from Sonia to confirm it.

I passed through the checkpoint and heard the old-timey sound of a calliope, which by some accident of irony was playing "Off We Go into the Wild Blue Yonder." The prison authorities insisted I put on a special "Returning Hearts" T-shirt, silkscreened on the front with a logo of two balloons—one red, one blue—floating over a black background cut through with strands of barbed wire. Balloons were temporary, of course, even to a child, but it occurred to me that to an inmate's child the sight of barbed wire would be lasting. Some inmates in such T-shirts were already playing basketball with their kids, also wearing the T-shirts, on temporary courts set up in the concessions area for the rodeo. It was all being filmed for a promotional video, and I saw now that the inmates and their children all wore primary colors—red, yellow, green, blue—while all the Christian volunteers wore gray, the color they'd given me. The calliope was now playing "The Man on the Flying Trapeze," the grounds set up like a midway with all kinds of games from some innocent era that never existed—a ring toss, a wooden cutout through which you threw baseballs, one of those devices where you swing a hammer and Test Your Own Strength. The T-shirts with their jumble of colors brought to mind gumballs in a machine. On the bleachers in the rodeo arena, inmates in these shirts sat in a tightly packed group, waiting, as an emcee, with the same ebullience as the emcee at the prison rodeo, bellowed out their names one by one over the PA system. *Ty-rone Young! Cal-vin Witherspoo-o-on!* Their kids came running out of a chute onto a patch of grass to greet them. One man's huge teenage daughter came at him at a full sprint—she was bigger than he was—and ended up tackling him to the ground. A tall man with a white towel around his neck stepped forward with no affect, then scooped up his two

daughters like pets and smilingly carried them off, one
on each shoulder. In the shade of the bleachers, the men
were frowning, intent, gripped by concern, wondering if
their child would even arrive, but as soon as their names
were called and they stepped out into the sunlight they
became vividly ordinary. I was sitting next to a man whose
sixteen-year-old daughter lived outside Baton Rouge, not
that far away, but he told me he'd got the news yesterday
that she wouldn't be here. She was on a track team and
suddenly it turned out there was a meet in Florida—that
was the story, though of course he knew there was more to
it. He'd decided to watch anyway, because he "just wanted
to see what the whole thing was like." The line of kids had
started to dwindle now, longer and longer pauses between
announcements. I saw some inmates I knew, and I waved
from a distance, but it was hard to talk, the jokes starting, the mood darkening. I didn't see Kendrick or Aysha
anywhere.

I'd become friendly with the assistant warden, Cathy,
who found me and asked if I wanted to go over to see
something called the Guardians Meeting, a gathering of
the mothers and grandparents and other relatives who had
driven the children here. They were in a building normally
used as a training center for corrections officers, where, beneath a banner that read NUTRITION 101, a woman was
giving a sparsely attended lecture about the health bene-
fits of positive thinking, asking if anyone kept a "gratitude
journal," then presenting her listeners with something she

called a Gratitude Box, a kind of piggy bank in which you
inserted thank-you notes for good things that happened in
your life. She stressed the importance of exercise, diet, vegetables. "Stop smoking," advised one of the women in the
audience, when asked if she knew of any other health tips.
There was something called a "sleep station," a "biomet-
ric screening room," a giant silver vat full of flour that you
could stuff into balloons to create "stress balls" to squeeze
during times of anxiety. There were plastic vegetables you
could load onto a plastic plate to see how much healthy food
equaled the caloric content of one small bag of McDonald's
fries. "Sometimes kids miss their moms and they have to
bring them over here," Cathy said. There was so much pressure, so many ways for it to go wrong. Beyond the nutrition
area, a young pastor from the nonprofit organization was
giving a talk about the event itself. "It's joyfully sad," he
said. "It's *awesome.* Thank you." He was young enough to
speak ironically without meaning anything ironic. *"Amen?"*
he asked, as if ironically. *Amen,* the audience said, because
there were only a few of them there and everything about
this place was disorienting and unfamiliar except for that
word.

I was still with Cathy when I first ran into Kendrick,
back on the fake midway, crowded now with fathers and
children playing carnival games, collecting play money
to exchange for prizes, food, stuffed animals, other toys.
Kendrick greeted me in a manner very different from any
other time we'd met, either because he was with Aysha or

because I was with Cathy. I tried to catch up to his effu-
siveness, which seemed almost hysterical. He was happy—
certainly that was part of it, standing there in his green
T-shirt with his daughter, whom he introduced to Cathy—
Miss Cathy, this my daughter, Aysha—and then Aysha, the sleeves
of her red T-shirt rolled up to make it more stylish, tilted
her shoulders to one side and with sleepy eyes extended her
hand toward Cathy, who after saying hi was offering hers
to shake. The tilted shoulders, the sleepy eyes—there was a
whole world of relationships in this moment that I struggled to understand, but Aysha grasped it immediately: I was
on Cathy's side against her and her father. It went back to
long before I'd even met either of them. I said hello, and
Aysha said hello back in a voice more mature than the voice
I'd heard in Houston, then I hugged her in the way of an
evangelical Christian who went through his whole life missing out on the joke.

"I never thought this day would come," Kendrick said,
smiling. "I just never believed it could really happen."

He put his arm around Aysha and kissed the top of her
head and she turned her face shyly toward his chest. Cathy's
phone had rung—it never stopped ringing—and she was
stepping away.

"I'm going for my ordination," Kendrick told me then.
"I been taking the classes for a while now. I never told you
about that."

Whatever mask he was wearing now was worn with
great poise.

"To become a minister," I said.

"It's what I want to do when I get back on the streets. It's what I got to set my mind on from here forward. 'If you desert God's law, you're free to embrace depravity; if you love God's law, you fight for it tooth and nail.' Tooth and nail, that's my focus now. The future. Or I'll put it like this: 'Justice makes no sense to the evil-minded.' I had to think about that one for a while. I had to think about that for a long time."

He was smiling, not accusatory, and I started to back away. Perhaps the smile was itself accusatory. I'd said I was surprised, but I was really only a little surprised—I knew at least three inmates who had become ordained ministers through the prison's Bible college. It was a way to pass the time, if nothing else, a way to keep one's mind alive. *It's what I want to do when I get back out on the streets.* I wondered how much time had passed between Aysha telling him she wanted to come visit and Kendrick enrolling in the classes.

"It's good to see you," I said.

"Always."

"I'll see you later, Aysha."

She looked at me and didn't say anything, still clinging to Kendrick.

When Cathy got off the phone, she and I walked toward the main prison, the inside of which I had never seen before. I was glad she hadn't commented on my familiarity

with Kendrick, with Aysha, but I realized my concern
about this failed to take into consideration my own insignificance. She was telling me now about her career as
a prison employee before she'd become a warden. She'd
started as a guard in a tower at another prison, a night shift
where there was nothing to do—no TV or books, a toilet
built right into the seat because you couldn't leave. There
was just the radio. "You grew to hate the few songs you
loved, and to really hate the other ones," she said. She said
there was a guy on that job who got so bored that he shot
a deer from his tower. Most of the corrections officers being hired now were women, she said, because they were
the only ones willing to work for such low pay. At night,
a single guard would be in charge of a dorm full of ninety
inmates. Recently, a woman guard had been found having
sex with one of the inmates within the first hour of her first
shift. She told me these things, and yet I almost never saw
any women guards.

"Keep your eyes straight ahead when we go inside," she
told me, as we were buzzed out of the gated vestibule we'd
been standing in, the wall of bars sliding open, then closing
shut behind us. "You'll see."

We walked down a long sidewalk beneath a white
overhang that protected us from the sun, then through
a metal door into the first dorm, which was Kendrick's.
She reminded me to keep my eyes straight ahead. It was
because there was a shower room to the right and there
was someone using it, a solitary nude figure in a sea of old

tile. As we kept walking, there were some stainless-steel
sinks, small mirrors hung above them at erratic angles, a
row of stainless-steel toilets without enclosures. The dorm
itself was silent. It contained columns of neatly made bunk
beds running the white length, drum fan at either end, the
dim, sedate light like the light of an airport. At the feet
and corners of each bed sat gray footlockers and laundry
bags made of pale green vinyl, more of these bags beneath
the beds, along with shower sandals and carefully arranged
shoes. Cathy showed me Kendrick's bunk—Kendrick's
two rolls of toilet paper, Kendrick's red toothbrush. There
were only two men in the dorm, both old, both sitting in
isolation on the edges of their beds, reading. They were
fully dressed and even wore shoes—it struck me that they
weren't lying down, which would have lessened the sense
of military order. At the far end of the dorm, there was a
day room, a dark enclosure behind glass with bare wooden
benches and a single TV. Another solitary man was watching a movie behind the glass. I could see from where I
stood that the movie happened to be set inside a prison.
He was sitting in a prison dorm, watching a violent fight
scene break out in an imaginary prison dorm. I don't know
what else goes on in such places. I don't mean the violence,
I mean the life of a prisoner who spends part of his life
watching a movie about prison. I asked Cathy about sex
and she said, "That's the big secret. That's what nobody
will talk about." Waking up every morning to find yourself
back in this dorm, the movement of the sun a way people

trick themselves into believing in time, the corridors connecting dorm to dorm made of cinder block the gray of
battleships, leading out to another day in the farm fields
or the chicken-processing plant or making furniture or
scrubbing floors. There was no such thing as time. There
was no such place as outside. Maybe you yourself were not
quite real. They could talk about rape, but not sex. Rape,
but not other human contact.

"I'm going to see if I can start writing to you," I told
Kendrick when I saw him again later that afternoon.

He'd been telling me about how his day was going with
Aysha. They'd talked about which TV shows she liked
(*Everybody Hates Chris, C.S.I.*) and she'd told him at some
point that he reminded her of a rapper he'd never heard of
and he'd smiled. She'd promised that she would tell him
before she started dating boys, that they would talk about
it on the phone. He wanted "to be there," he said, did not
want to be just "a weekend dad," but what we really talked
about in this brief moment was not Aysha but what had
happened on Athena Street. I asked him again about the
murder, and he told me again all the things he'd told me
before, with some clarifications. As always, we were in full
view of other people and as always there was not enough
time to catch up to what he was really saying or conceal-
ing or why he was doing either. When I asked if Athena
Street was a place to score drugs, for example, he said that it

"occurred" but that it wasn't that common—it wasn't why he used to go there. He said that he mostly went there because of his cousin Mason, who was "friends with those people." He said that maybe the murder wasn't even about drugs. We were talking just before the closing ceremony, as Kendrick and Aysha and all the other fathers and children in their rainbow-colored T-shirts were gathering in the arena, the crowd pushing tighter and tighter toward the center, Aysha so strongly impelled onward that she could hardly wait up for Kendrick as she sought a better place in the bleachers. I was glad we were talking about practicalities, back to something like common ground, but now Aysha turned toward us, holding a stuffed tiger that had some sort of emblem stitched in purple into its side, and Kendrick finally rejoined her. I sat in the bleachers far behind them, trying again to understand what alchemy of tone and body language always enabled him to give the impression of such total self-assurance. On our way into the arena, we'd been handed little green cards printed with a circle surrounded by a ring, the circle labeled 1 CORINTHIANS 15:3–4, and around it, the ring divided into four quadrants: GOD John 3:16, TRUST Acts 16:31, MAN Romans 3:23, CROSS Romans 5:8. *I'm going for my ordination. I been taking the classes for a while now. I never told you about that.* Onstage, a preacher was talking about the resurrection. By way of illustration, he used a parable about an inmate he'd met here who'd managed to build a working guitar from scraps of a broken-down piano. "How impressive these prisoners are," he said. "How surprising." After calling upon his audience to testify to their faith, he encouraged all the "dads" out there to turn to their kids and pray, to "be the spiritual leaders that many of you are." Most of the men continued to simply linger with their children during this silence, but Kendrick was among the tiny group I saw who actually recited the words on the green card, pointing them out to Aysha with his finger as he read. *For all have sinned and fall short of the glory of God. For the wages of sin is death, but the gift of God is eternal life in Christ Jesus our Lord.* There was nothing in the simplifications on the green card that shed any light on how Kendrick persevered. I knew less and less the more I watched.

"You be good," he told me at the end of the ceremony. "God bless you."

"It's none of my business, these things I've been asking you about. I hope you know I understand that."

"I told you the truth. I always was. It's just complicated. It's what I told you at the very beginning."

"I know. Whenever we talk, I do know that."

They'd solicited everyone's pledge to accept Christ—Aysha had not been able to raise her hand, and perhaps anticipating this Kendrick had not raised his. Then the volunteers released dozens of white balloons in celebration of the covenant they'd proposed. The balloons now floated above Kendrick's head into the sky above the arena, then out toward the fences, the barbed wire, the towers, the fields. When I looked in Aysha's eyes to say goodbye, I saw a wild blankness this time. It was as if in just the last few minutes everything had changed. *Everybody Hates Chris, C.S.I.*— her father at this former slave planation set up to look like a county fair. Perhaps the prison had finally revealed itself as so specific and alien that it had made him seem unknowable. No sooner had he been given back to her than he'd been taken away.

14

It turned out that it was Marcus, Kendrick's brother, who had driven Aysha to Angola—I met him the following day, Sunday, at Sonia's house, the house on the West Bank she planned to leave to Kendrick and Marcus as her legacy. My first impression of Marcus was his rented SUV: impassive, almost too large for the driveway, immaculately parked with its side mirrors pushed back. There was something strict or pragmatic about Marcus in person that made it hard for me to guess what, if anything, he felt about meeting me. He didn't look like Kendrick. He wore eyeglasses and a green golf shirt that hung loosely around his thin arms but clung more tightly around his small potbelly. It wasn't that he was large like his SUV, it was that its largeness was under his control. He told me later that he was thirty-eight, that he lived in Harlem—"you know, one of those gentrifying places"— and when he said this I couldn't tell if he was inviting me to join him in some knowing irony, or if he was anticipating some knowing irony on my part that he didn't share. Sonia's

house had a comfortably air-conditioned living room, but
he preferred to sit in the long screened-in porch off the back
side, where even in the shade and with a standing fan I was
sweating a little. That was where we talked, among the mis-
matched plastic chairs, some stacked with newspapers and
magazines, each of us with a large plastic glass of iced tea
poured from a cardboard carton. I asked him how he'd decided to become an architect, and he said that when he was
in his early twenties, he was living in Brooklyn with one of
his uncles, his mother's brother-in-law, who was a master
electrician, and because Marcus had dropped out of high
school and had "no real direction at that time," he became
his uncle's apprentice. After a year or two, he found a better-
paying job working for Con Edison. One day, by chance,
his crew was dispatched to a hospital in Manhattan where
the power had gone out. The sense of urgency caused him
to think a very obvious thought, he said, which is that hos-
pitals are intricate and important buildings. That was how
he became an architect, he told me. Within a month of the
Con Ed service call, he'd enrolled himself in a GED pro-
gram, then took the SAT and got a scholarship to Brooklyn
College. After that, he went directly to get his master's in
architecture at UCLA.

"You don't have to look like that," he said. "Like it's
some incredible story. It's actually a pretty ordinary story."

I asked if he was the first person in his family to go to
college, and he nodded.

"I went, but Kendrick might have been smarter than me
in some ways," he said. "You see that sometimes, the younger

one smarter than the older. They have it easier. The oldest gets the rules, the discipline, the fear."

Aysha hadn't come out of her room since I'd arrived, about forty minutes ago. I'd come mostly to see her, because I knew her visit with her father the day before had been confusing, among other things, and that it must have been strange to be spending several days with family members you hadn't seen in many years (if in fact she had ever seen her uncle Marcus before at all). Sonia had invited me over, and as always she had been cheerful when she greeted me—pouring Marcus and me the iced teas, apologizing that there wasn't much else in the house, offering me a slice of the coffee cake I'd brought over—and as always I'd felt alert in the face of her cheerfulness, unable to quite answer it with my own. I wondered about Aysha, who seemed to be hiding. Sitting on that hot porch with Marcus now, I waited for a moment when I could excuse myself to go see if she'd come out of her room.

Kendrick, he was saying now, "probably could have gotten a scholarship." He was "pretty good at basketball," a shooting guard, but maybe the rigor of high school sports had "turned him off, because he never pursued that. He was sweet-tempered, but not a competitive type of person. That might have been one of the problems he had, if you start looking back in a certain way. I remember him and his cousin Mason, they wanted to be cops, or gangsters—it kept changing. There was this sort of a superhero movie they watched, *The Crow*, it had a black cop in it. Kendrick had memorized all the lines this cop would say. Maybe they were fourteen or fifteen at that time. I think Kendrick and Mason are pretty much the same age."

He went on about Kendrick and Mason, always referring to Mason as "Kendrick's cousin," as though he weren't his own cousin too, as though they weren't all equally related. Kendrick and Mason, Kendrick and Mason—all the "foolishness" the two of them got involved in as boys and adolescents. He said that Mason spent many summers in New Orleans—his mother, their aunt Terri, lived in Los Angeles and Mason was too much for her, even though he was "really just a sweet kid, not a mean bone in his body, more of a clown type—a court jester type." He and Kendrick had a game they played where they would slap each other's open palms until their hands were so pulpy and swollen they had to ice them afterward. Kendrick broke his arm in one of their stunt fights—"maybe five hundred dollars, that stupidity cost my mother." The same summer, Mason got hit by a car on his bike and "never walked right again." It was all a joke to them, as if they were in some phase where they perceived their bodies as only half real, half cartoon. It was almost like they had a kind of private language they spoke, Marcus said, but maybe it just seemed that way to him, because he was "out of it," older, and didn't really understand.

"I'm talking about the early days," he said. "A long time ago."

Hip-hop, action movies, "those little BMX bikes—the shit they would buy." His face looked grave, though the examples of Kendrick and Mason's "foolishness" didn't seem grave to me. I remembered the day I'd first met Sonia, not here but at the spotless house owned by her coworker in Carville, where during our conversation in the living room she'd told me about Kendrick teaching himself to speak Spanish so that he could make friends with kids in the neighborhood who didn't speak English. It was too cute a story to be fully true, the kind of story a boy tells his mother to persuade her that he's more innocent than he really is, but though a part of me had doubted the story, another part of me had wanted to believe it enough that I'd passed it on to Aysha the first night I met her in Houston. It occurred to me now that Sonia had invited me to the house today for a reason, perhaps unconsciously, and that the reason was that she and Marcus had been telling half-truths to each other about Kendrick for years, benignly or not. Perhaps she wanted someone to witness these half-truths, even if no one would ever be able to mention it out loud. As Marcus continued to reminisce about his and Kendrick's childhood, I wondered if he even knew his brother. I asked him if he was aware of the arrests Kendrick had had before the murder on Athena Street, and he said no, he'd had no idea about that. What about drugs? I asked. No, he didn't know anything about drugs either, though it didn't "sound like Kendrick." I asked him if he knew that Kendrick had spent ten days in Orleans Parish Prison less than a week before the murder, and again he said he hadn't known about that. If it was true, he said, it was "difficult to believe."

"I was working hard, every single day," he said then. "New York, Los Angeles—Boston, where I had my first job. I would call home and hear from my mother about some

foolishness Kendrick got up to. Kendrick stopped going
to school. Or Kendrick's going to be a daddy. He's back in
school, he's out of school, he got a job, he lost the job. I can't
really explain how that affected me. Six years—six and a
half years, really—that was how long it took to get the GED,
go through undergrad, grad, get the accreditation. I worked
in Boston, then I moved back to New York, and every single
day through all that time I was working hard. Very hard. If
you're scared of heights, they say, don't look down. That's
what I mean. I wasn't trying to look down. Because when
I heard Kendrick was facing those charges—I knew what
would happen. I knew he was innocent, but I knew what
was going to happen anyway. And I couldn't deal with it. I
probably still can't, if I'm honest with you. I was angry that
he even allowed himself to get in that position. Still angry."

He looked down into his plastic cup, and something
about his face suggested to me an echo of what his father's
face might have looked like, though I'd never seen his father's face. He didn't look like Sonia—Kendrick looked
more like Sonia—so I gathered that he must look more
like his father, though it seemed that it was Sonia's per-
sistence and drive that had got him through architecture
school, just as it had enabled her to purchase this house.
When I asked him about his father, he said he hadn't heard
from him in ten years—since the year of Kendrick's trial.
It was a story for another time, he told me. He said that
he had no family of his own in New York, no spouse, no
children. He'd lost touch with the uncle in Brooklyn who
had trained him as an electrician. We look for cues about

people we don't know. We make assumptions about them
in order to navigate the world, moment by moment, imagining them before we know them, which of course is just
prejudice, and this was the way I'd encountered Marcus,
who I was now trying to see more clearly. We sat there on
the hot screened-in porch and eventually I accepted that I
wasn't getting any closer. Another time, he repeated, and
we sat there for another few moments in silence, then went
back into the house.

I knocked on Aysha's door. I could hear the muffled sounds
of her voice, talking to herself, it seemed at first, but then
almost as though there were someone else with her in the
room. She started laughing, still not answering me. I'd
brought her a gift, a graphic novel, but it seemed young for
her now, or perhaps just too mild. When I called out her
name, she laughed again at something, then yelled "hold on"
and went back to her strange or imaginary conversation, her
voice quiet at first, then more boisterous.

"She's texting on her phone," Sonia said to me, when I
came back to the living room. "She texts, but then she reads
most of it out loud anyway."

She was lying on an L of the black sofa, her shoes off,
legs straight out before her, an empty plate on her stomach, the TV on. It was her day off. She'd had to work yesterday, which was why she hadn't been able to go to the
prison with Aysha and Marcus.

"That phone—it's just a new toy her uncle bought her.

They had a big day yesterday. I'm glad she got to see her father, though. That they got to see each other."

"She got to see you, too."

"That's right. And I'm grateful for that as well."

"I brought her a little gift. Maybe you can give it to her for me."

"Of course."

I put the gift down on the coffee table, then leaned over and gave her a hug goodbye.

As I was opening my car door out on the street, Marcus stopped me. He'd been standing at the side of his SUV, searching for something inside the truck's cabin, it looked like, and when I called out goodbye, he looked up and said goodbye back, but now he seemed to have changed his mind and wanted to talk. He took a few steps forward into Sonia's yard, his hands crossed before his waist, and I thought for a moment that there was more tension between us than I'd imagined, but in fact he was asking me if I had a few minutes to go for a ride.

"Maybe fifteen minutes," he said. "Just over to Algiers. There's something I want to show you, really just some buildings is all."

We ended up going together in his truck. He kept one of those folding cardboard screens across the windshield, but it was nevertheless stifling when we got inside. The interior was immaculately clean, the leather passenger seat so wide and smooth it was difficult to sit in comfortably. He and Aysha had driven close to six hours yesterday, but there was not a single empty can or bottle or wrapper left from that

journey. He followed Route 90 east, which I realized was
the same route Kendrick would have taken when he drove
from Janelle's trailer to Antoinette's apartment on Athena
Street almost eleven years ago on the night of the murder. I wondered how much Marcus even knew about any
of that. As always, I felt uneasy knowing so much that was
none of my business, and this unease was compounded now
by the sense that Marcus, who hadn't even come home for
Kendrick's trial, understood more about his brother than I
ever could.

We got off the highway just before the Crescent City
Connection bridge, then he made a left and a right turn
and began to slow down on L. B. Landry Boulevard in an
isolated corner of the neighborhood of Algiers. The radio
was playing an R&B song with comic Arab and Latin flour-
ishes, the music so incongruous with the general mood that
I looked at Marcus to see how it registered on his face, but
he didn't seem to be listening. He started looking for parking. The streets were laid out as in an ordinary suburban
subdivision, but the area was right up against the highway
overpass, and there was a telltale blandness I recognized
from other parts of the city. I knew that it was with devel-
opments like this one that the Housing Authority of New
Orleans had replaced the city's old housing projects after
Katrina. They'd put up these cheerful new buildings in different colors, styles, and sizes, renting many of them out at
market rates, and thereby reducing the amount of publicly
subsidized housing by as much as two thirds. The block we
were on now was almost empty, but for some reason Marcus

decided to park on the side of the one street where there
were other cars. He did it meticulously, first pulling in behind a black Chevy, then deciding that he wasn't straight
enough, then starting all over again by parallel parking, ma-
neuvering the huge truck back and forth many times until
he was satisfied.

He sat there for a moment, his hands still on the
wheel, the engine running. He told me that this had been
the Fischer Projects, a name I recognized from inmates at
Angola who'd grown up here. The block we were on now,
Marcus said, was where he and his mother and father had
once lived. They'd lived there until he was seven, a year after
Kendrick was born. The Fischer Projects had housed more
than two thousand people back then, he said, as opposed to
the nine hundred or so who'd managed to come back since
the storm. He described the old architecture: the gray brick
façades with narrow windows, the repetitive apartment
blocks set at zigzag angles to each other so that you could see
a wedge of red brick on their sides. There'd been a thirteen-
story high-rise where elderly people lived and fourteen low-
rise structures set in those zigzag rows—"like on a military
base," he said, pointing out the window. That was where he
and his mother and Kendrick had lived—his father, he said,
had really only been there off and on during that time.

"My uncle, my father's brother, lived here too," he said,
gesturing out toward some houses across from an empty
playground. "My uncle Sherwin. Not the uncle in Brooklyn,
a different one. My uncle Sherwin died of a heroin overdose
when I was six. It was the same year Kendrick was born.

Like I said, we moved a year after that, when Kendrick was one and I was seven. That was the first time we went to Brooklyn. My mother had relatives up there, so that's where we went."

He kept looking out the windshield straight ahead, his fingers moving a little on the steering wheel, waiting. He finally explained that two years before his uncle Sherwin died, a white cop had been found shot to death in the Fischer Projects. Over the next few nights, a group of other cops terrorized the neighborhood, torturing people, Marcus said, including his uncle Sherwin, whom they picked up at random. They drove him to an empty lot near the river levee and while he was handcuffed they beat him for more than two hours. Other "suspects" were beaten in jail cells, or hit with phone books while chained to a chair, or threatened at gunpoint, or nearly asphyxiated by plastic bags tied over their heads. I could read all about this if I wanted, he said, I could just do an Internet search on "Algiers Seven," which is what the cops were called in the press. Out of their "interrogations" came false information that led them to four innocent people whom they tracked down and killed: three black men and one black woman, whom they shot while she was in the bathtub. The police were never convicted of these killings. Two years later, Marcus said, his uncle Sherwin died of a heroin overdose. There was no way to know what, if anything, he'd told the cops during his beating.

"To my mind, he was killed by the same cops who killed those four other people," he said. "To my father's mind, his brother was murdered by those cops. He was never the same after that, my father. Like I said, we moved to Brooklyn a year after that. We moved in with my auntie and uncle, tried to start a new life, but there was a recession, it was 1983—there were no jobs, the streets were dangerous, what we got was a crowded apartment in Crown Heights with police sirens at night. Bad luck. Bad timing. My mother did better with it than my father did. My father went silent. Silent or yelling, when he was with my mother. You didn't want to be around when he was there, but most of the time he wasn't. That was the first time we moved to Brooklyn."

His father had ended up working as an informal tax preparer, he told me then. He didn't know if he still did that anymore, because they hadn't spoken in so long, but when they left Brooklyn and came back to New Orleans, he said, his father started doing people's taxes. He'd taught himself math and financial accounting, though, like Marcus, he'd dropped out of high school. The business went well sometimes, but sometimes his father didn't collect his fees, because he wasn't "hard" and would settle for promises or barter. For years, Marcus said, he'd thought of his father as a frustrated man who drank too much and avoided his family. It was only when he got older, he said, that he realized that this way of thinking only reduced himself to the son of a stereotype. Did I know what that was like, he asked, and I said that maybe I understood it better than he thought. We sat in silence for a while. I finally asked if he knew about the book I'd written about my own father, and he said no, he didn't. I told him a little about it, the short version, which is lurid, and then I said that the story was complicated, that the book had failed in a sense because I'd underestimated these complications and people's need to form judgments. When I'd looked at the complications, I'd seen that in the end my father's friends had been mostly right about him: there was something hidden, but there wasn't crookedness, there wasn't criminality. But in spite of my efforts to portray him this way credibly, there were readers who came away thinking that my father somehow deserved what had happened to him. My father was shot to death in a garage because he gave testimony against a man who could hire someone to do that. My father knew that kind of man, in other words. I can never tell his story without feeling that accusation from the person I'm telling it to, and I felt it now in the truck with Marcus. It's partly the blood, the indecency of it, and it's partly the problem of sympathy, which I don't want. It's partly the identification of myself with my father's killing. That's the kind of person I am, the kind who would have a father that that happened to.

"I didn't know about that," Marcus said.

"I thought maybe Sonia had told you."

"No, she didn't. I don't think she did."

We got out of the truck and walked down the street toward the empty playground, which was covered in mulch, not grass. At the center of the playground stood a jungle gym painted the New Orleans colors of purple, yellow, and green, surrounded by unused benches. Because there were so few cars, trees, or fences, you could see a wide swath of houses, and because it was so empty it began to look more and more to me like a photograph of a crime scene. It was about two o'clock in the afternoon and the only human presence in the whole subdivision was a few young men hanging out either by themselves or in a small group a few blocks down from the playground. As I said, I knew the history of this place. It was where one of the inmates I'd interviewed became a contract killer while he was still in his teens. He'd raised pit bulls, had been a boxer—"I always felt I was capable of killing someone," he'd told me, and the first time he killed someone he was paid ten thousand dollars for it. The money "was coming in bulk," he said, but he was always on guard, always in hiding. By the time he was arrested, he'd killed more than thirty people. He was twenty-three. The ghosts of that time were still palpable as we stood there on the playground.

"The corner store used to be called Julian's," Marcus told me now. "I was only six, seven years old, but I remember that. Julian's. Hanging at Julian's, getting your drink on. Of course, that's the scene that was waiting for me. We moved, we got out, but still, I know Kendrick had problems when he was growing up. I knew a lot of what was going on with him in those days. You didn't have to tell me all that—the arrests, the jail time. That happens. I get it now, thirty-seven years old, the cops still in my face. I'm just saying you need to understand. Sometimes it's better to say you didn't know there were problems like that. Because if you start explaining, you'd never stop."

I knew almost nothing about Marcus, apart from these few things he'd been telling me about his education and his family. If I had to guess, I found myself thinking, I'd say he was a Republican, but I knew this was simply my interpretation of his stiffness, which reminded me of certain military people I'd met. It was my interpretation of the green golf shirt he was wearing, its fabric shining in the sunlight, sweat stains at the underarms. He was examining the buildings now—the windows' ersatz panes, the fiber cement siding, the roof shingles that were already shifting a little—walking slowly up to a few of the houses. He was calm, surveying the area with a scrutiny that derived from his training. It was still the projects, he said to me then. It looked all right now, but what happened when the sills rotted out, or the beadboard, or the whole thing needed to be repainted? The history of public housing was that the cost of maintenance was unsustainable. I asked him if he remembered where exactly he'd lived here and he said he wasn't sure, it was all different now, just houses on ordinary streets, and back then you didn't think about streets but "courts"—the buildings were gray monoliths divided into courts with institutional names. Even as a child, you felt them as a kind of experiment designed by people far away who had set it all up and forgotten about it. Algiers was in the Fifteenth Ward, he said. You called it the One-Five. There was a special kind of heroin sold there called One-Five.

It was too hot to stay outside for long. We took a last look at what had been erased—the thirteen-story tower for the elderly, the low-rise institutional buildings in their zigzag rows—then we walked back toward the SUV. I must have been daydreaming, because it took me a while as I stood there outside the passenger door to realize that Marcus hadn't followed me all the way. I didn't see him on the other side of the truck, and I had to walk around the rear in order to find him standing across the street from me, his hands on his hips. I raised my chin as if to ask what was going on, but he didn't speak. It was as if he were still looking for the old buildings.

When we got back to Sonia's house, I went inside for a glass of water and that was when I finally saw Aysha, sitting at the kitchen table. She had a slice of the coffee cake I'd brought over on a plate before her, and she was trying to eat it with her fingers while typing on her phone. We said hello to each other but she didn't look up to make eye contact. She was still wearing the red "Returning Hearts" T-shirt from the day before, the one with the balloons and barbed wire on it, and it had the stretched, wrinkled look of having been slept in. In general, she looked like she'd just got out of bed, though it was almost three in the afternoon.

"You're going to ruin your screen," I said.

I had filled a glass of water from the sink and now I drank from it. Whether she'd gotten my gift or not, I didn't know. All she cared about, of course, was the phone. She asked me for my number and I gave it to her and when she finished typing it in, she showed me her screen so I could verify it. I noticed that instead of my name, she'd entered a row of emojis: round yellow faces with beetle-browed expressions.

"Is that how you do all your contacts?" I asked.

She took the phone back.

"You gave me the Old Fart emoji," I said. "Why don't you call me, so I can have your number too?"

I doubted she would contact me, nor did I think I would contact her, but I told her she could if she wanted. She pressed the call button and hung up before I answered.

"Your father has a tattoo," I said. "You know the one I'm talking about? It's on his arm. The six-pointed star. Did he ever tell you about it?"

"No."

"The next time you talk to him you should ask him about it. Ask him what it means."

"I don't really care."

"No?"

She licked her fingers and looked back down at her phone.

"Your phone have a New Orleans area code or a Houston area code?" I asked.

"New Orleans. Five-oh-four, baby."

She did a little halfhearted fist pump, mocking me. I remembered that poem we'd worked on together in Houston, "Solace," Aysha in her plaid school uniform, seemingly a different person then. I had a picture on my own phone that I showed her. It was of my half sister, whom I'd met only five years ago. I told Aysha that my father, before he met my mother, had had a child with another woman. That was my half sister, the woman in the photo. She'd been put up for adoption. I didn't know anything about her until

I published my book about my father and she found it. I asked Aysha if she knew about that book of mine, and unlike Marcus, she said yes, she did, her mother had told her about it. I explained to her then that I had another half sibling, a half brother, whom I had known all my life—he and I had always been very close, I admired him more than anyone I knew, but when I began working on the book about our father, he grew distant. When the book finally came out, he stopped speaking to me. I said that that was the "bad thing" about writing the book. I said that the "good thing" about it was that my half sister had found out about it and contacted me. She'd been trying to locate me for many years, but had never known how. I didn't know if I believed my half sister at first, but then I asked her to send me a photograph of herself and I saw right away that she was telling the truth: she was obviously my father's daughter. If I hadn't written the book, I said, I would never have met her.

I said that you never know what will happen when you start looking at the past: it's frightening for a reason. I hoped she understood that she and her father had a lot of past between them still to look at. I didn't tell her that my half brother had died in an accident three years ago, that we'd never had a chance to reconcile. I softened the story, turning it into a homily about a "bad thing" and a "good thing" that came out of "looking at the past." The further I went with the story, the less I understood why I was telling it to her.

15

Aysha's red prison T-shirt, Marcus's green golf shirt, Sonia lying on the black sofa with an empty plate on her stomach, the jungle gym painted the New Orleans colors of purple, yellow, and green—my mind was full of images as I got into my car to drive back home. I'd been listening and talking too much and it had given me a mild headache, so I told myself to be patient as I situated myself in the driver's seat, but the more deliberate I was—closing the door, putting on my seatbelt, fitting the key into the ignition—the more difficult it became to tell how slow or fast I was actually moving. I turned the key and my sight was briefly occluded by white disks, like nested moons. The disks separated, then dissolved, then lingered as a few twirling sparks at the periphery of my vision. It was something that had been happening to me for a few months now, brief spells of dizziness and disorientation, though usually only when I first woke up. I rocked forward a little. I'd been concerned about these "spells" and what they might mean, though while they were happening I just wanted to move deeper into the unsteadiness. *If you're scared of heights, they say, don't look down,* Marcus had said. The momentary lapses felt like a way of testing how far I could look down without falling off some edge, as if I thought they might teach me something. Perhaps the voice in my head that said I was falling, for example, or the voice that said I wanted to fall, was just noise.

The car was running. I looked for a moment at the dashboard, then touched the steering wheel with my fingertips, not gripping it. My half brother had stopped speaking to me because of the book I'd written about our father. Perhaps the opposite of seeing things in black and white is imagining swirls of light that aren't there. I'd made our father into a "character" in a "story," made myself a character in a story; it was my way of replacing a simple truth—that our father hadn't deserved what had happened to him—with complications about how and why it had happened anyway. At home, in a manila envelope, I had photographs from the Old Records Office of the crime scene at Athena Street—pictures of the bullet wounds in Damien Martin's head, pictures of his blood on the kitchen walls. I had the transcripts and recordings of Kendrick's statements to the police and folders and notebooks full of information about his legal case. "You cannot hold back and be shy," the photographer Mary Ellen Mark once said. "You have to feel a situation; not hurt someone, not aggress someone to the point that it's obnoxious, but accept the fact that you are a voyeur—you're stealing something from people." Perhaps making people's lives into stories is a way of avoiding their actuality, or denying it—imagining swirls of light that aren't there. I knew if I ever started writing about Kendrick, he would become a "character," I would become a character, and these likenesses, no matter how grounded in fact, would be fictions, approximations, versions among other versions. I knew this was inevitable when you made portraits, even with a camera. "All photographs are accurate," Richard Avedon said. "None of them is the truth."

I drove east on Route 90, the same way I'd gone with Marcus to Algiers, the long overpass looking out on billboards and fast-food signs and the tops of palm trees that could have been many places in the South. I still felt dizzy, at a distance from things, and I told myself to pay more attention to the road, but I kept thinking. The voices inside my head were just noise, I told myself, a story I kept narrating moment by moment to try to get the world to fit back into my idea of it. I wrote stories about other people in order to break out of this nothingness. Out of my ignorance. The alternative was to turn away, to retreat back into the privilege of being able to turn away.

I passed by a sign for Stumpf Boulevard, and the street's name brought to mind a story I'd heard from a man who'd told it to me in the parking lot of Athena Street when I'd gone there to visit the crime scene. The apartment complex had been repainted pale yellow like some of the buildings Marcus and I had just seen on the site of the old Fischer Projects, but I had been to Athena Street before, when the brickwork was still covered in black mold and people gathered in the parking lots and at the sides of the buildings to use and sell drugs. It was run-down like that when a man told me his story about Stumpf Boulevard. He said that one night he and his girlfriend were at a tavern on Stumpf Boulevard and when they came out they saw a man passed out beneath his truck and they decided to help. They tried to revive him, and he suddenly sprang upright, screaming, his face covered in blood. The girlfriend saw police lights then, and they decided they should leave, but the cops pursued them. The man with the bloody face was in the backseat of the cop car now. He claimed it was the couple who had assaulted him. The man who told me the story ended up spending nine months in jail for this. He lost his job, his apartment, his car, all because he'd tried to help someone. *You go, you sit, they let you out,* he told me. *It's like school that way, you know.*

I wasn't paying attention to the road. I was thinking about that man in his sweatpants and undershirt and shower sandals. As I approached the exit sign for Terry Parkway, I came back into the present for a moment: Terry Parkway would have taken me to the Oakwood mall, and just beyond the mall was the turn for Athena Street. What Mary Ellen Mark had meant, of course, was that she had to push beyond questions of "right" and "wrong" and accept that she was the kind of person who was going to do what she wanted anyway. I'd been to Athena Street three times. Across the road from Damien Martin's former apartment there was a row of trees covered in thick vines, one of them like a hooded figure pointing its finger in accusation. I thought of the bullet wounds in the side of Damien Martin's forehead. *I'll pay-for-it, I'll pay-for-it, I'll pay-for-it, I'll pay-for-it. If I want it, if I want it, if I want it, if I want it* . . . The music in the car was like little pulses of white light, green light, plastic bulbs arrayed on a black grid. I wasn't going to turn the music down, because I didn't want to admit it was distracting me. *It's like school that way, you know.*

I was almost to the Crescent City Connection, the big openwork span that crosses the Mississippi River. A year or two ago, they'd stopped charging a toll, so there were booths now with no one manning them. The booths had no barricades, you just passed through the empty gaps, which were ghostly. I slowed down while wondering why I was slowing down. It felt strange to go through the toll plaza so fast. The old booths were beige concrete, reminiscent of military checkpoints. I was dizzy again, and as I rode up the rise of the bridge, I felt that my momentum would keep building and that it would carry me over the guardrail off the side. I could see the roadway widening and curving outward, and though I was steering straight, I could see myself veering harder and harder toward the rail and the gleaming river beyond it. I slowed down but there was traffic and I didn't want to cause an accident. I realized I had almost no control of the car. The only way I made it across the bridge was by trusting the position of my hands over the evidence of my eyes. I had to pull over when I was on the other side.

PART FOUR

BLINDNESS

16

Damien Wayne Martin, DOB 8-16-61. 14 Athena St, apt 5.

Body discovered 4 or 5 pm. Maintenance worker for building got into Martin's apartment with a tire tool.

Detectives found faint muddy shoe prints near front door, plus two partial bloody footprints in kitchen. Martin was found lying parallel to dishwasher and cabinets, his left knee (bent) resting against dishwasher, dressed in black T-shirt, jeans, white socks, black athletic shoes, lots of blood on floor. A black fishing style hat was on the kitchen counter next to the microwave with a bullet hole and bloodstain on the fabric. A sliding glass door at rear of kitchen was propped open by a wooden broomstick, the curtains closed.

In the upstairs bedroom, detectives found 6 live

British cartridges in top dresser drawer, 6 Winchester
.40 caliber cartridges, and a box containing 35 .380
cartridges. No weapons or narcotics were found.

—from Jefferson Parish Sheriff's Narrative,
item F-94857-02

17

About a mile from where I live is the St. Roch Cemetery, an expanse of white stone and whitewashed walls—white crypts, white headstones, urns, crosses, pillars, white angels gone gray with age. There are glass vases full of plastic and silk flowers—chrysanthemums, irises, roses, poinsettia. There's the bright white body of Christ made even whiter because it's hanging from a jet-black cross.

Out of the sun, I stood in the silence of the chapel, surprised to have forgotten what it was like, the vaulted ceiling and half the walls painted robin's-egg blue, the rest the pale cream of clouds. The altarpiece was made of carved wood with crocketed spires and had two paintings, one so darkened with age you could hardly see it, the other a bleached-out scene of Christ, a priest, an angel, two clouds full of cherubim. Before the altar stood the statue of St. Roch with his wide-brimmed hat, beard, cloak, and boots, his dog at his heels. He was the patron saint of dogs—also of falsely accused people, of plague victims, of healing. It was winter,

about ten months after that day at Sonia's house when I'd
first met Marcus. I had thought I would try to stop thinking about Kendrick and his story. The chapel now struck
me as a kind of reminder of all the gaps I had filled in after
thinking I had given up thinking about it. I remembered
a brass band that used to play every Thursday night in our
neighborhood bar when I first moved there, for I had moved
there at first by myself, while Sarah finished at her old job.
The bar had mobiles hanging from the ceiling in the shape
of sperm and the walls behind the cigarette smoke were a
dark, deliberately infernal red. It was August and so hot
that in the daytime the city looked abandoned. On those
Thursday nights, the band played with such force that I
couldn't hear afterward, the dancers rolling on the floor, the
horns a frenzy of joy. That band and others like it played in
the streets most Sunday afternoons, shutting down traffic
even on major thoroughfares so that a parade of often more
than a thousand people could meander the city, following a
club in matching brightly colored suits, with sashes, painted
umbrellas, giant feathered fans, before them a few floats for
the King and Queen, all of this in celebration of itself and
nothing else. Someday I would like to describe the beauty
of the brass bands, the parades on Sunday, all the ugliness
they overcome, but for now I was still preoccupied by the
thought that somewhere in the margins of those crowds
there was another Kendrick, another Lawrence Jeffries, another Damien Martin. When I used to come home after
those Thursday nights, it would be late and I would walk in
the middle of the street to keep an eye out for what might be

concealed by the parked cars and the trees. Armed robberies were common, police lights were common. The violence of what had happened to my father all those years ago had always felt distant from me, ungraspable, but it felt closer on those nights, penetrating my numbness and denial. I had stopped looking at my notes on Kendrick's story for ten months because I thought I didn't need to feel that way anymore. I thought I'd already spent too much of my life preoccupied by violence at the expense of what most people I knew thought of as ordinary.

I took a closer look at the altar, where people had placed a few offerings: a cross made of wrought iron, some pennies, a Mexican peso, a filbert nut, some Mardi Gras beads, a plastic doubloon on which someone had written in Sharpie *2015 World Champ*. I had stopped trying to make sense of these things by now. On my left was a primitive brown statue of a forlorn woman holding a Bible. On my right was a plaster statue of St. Lucy, its caramel-colored glaze cracking off in a vitiligo of white blotches. At my feet, the body of Christ lay in a glass case, blood trickling from beneath his crown of thorns and from the spear wound between his ribs. I had interviewed Kendrick's cousin Mason a few weeks before this. Sonia had thought that Mason would be in Los Angeles, where his mother lived, where he'd spent most of his childhood and adolescence, but Sonia had just lost track of him. When I called Mason's mother, Sonia's sister, she told me that Mason was in Meridian, Mississippi, and when I asked her why, she said only that he had friends there. She didn't want to talk to me, but she gave me his phone number, which turned out to be the number of a group home. I left a message there. It took me several tries to finally get in touch with Mason. He told me that he'd just gotten out of prison—five years in the East Mississippi Correctional Facility for his second heroin-possession offense. His sentence had been ten, he said, but they'd granted him parole, and so he'd just been released about six months ago. He had a kind of square face with a pencil mustache—I found his picture online, his mugshot—and though he was only twenty-five in the picture he looked ten years older than that. I found another image of him, an ad for a party-promotion venture he'd started in Jackson before his conviction. Freedom—Mason's and mine. *Accept the fact that you're a voyeur—you're stealing something from people.* Looking back over my notes after all that time, I'd realized that Kendrick had told me that it was Mason who'd first made friends with the people on Athena Street. They were Mason's friends before they were Kendrick's, in other words—he knew them longer, probably better. I also saw in my notes that someone, probably Kendrick, had made a phone call from Janelle's trailer a little after 10:45 on the morning of Damien Martin's murder, which happened not long afterward. One of the first things Mason said to me when I finally reached him was that he knew Kendrick was innocent—he knew this because he had talked to Kendrick on the phone that morning when Kendrick had called him. No one who knew Kendrick, he said, had any doubt that he was innocent.

An ex-voto is an offering made in gratitude, especially in gratitude for healing. At the side of the chapel, past the statue of St. Lucy, was a little alcove with peeling paint full of ex-votos that you could see behind an iron gate shaped like a gothic arch. There were plaster effigies of feet, legs, hands, and hearts that hung from the walls, along with old leg braces, prosthetics, orthopedic boots. There was a kind of corset made of white plastic in the shape of shoulders and an upper chest with an overhanging loop that fit over the head. It looked medieval even though I knew it was just an antiquated medical device. Plastic sunflowers, a bird's wing, lilies, roses, a pink stuffed poodle, pink angel wings. There was a toy vampire bat and a plaster puppy and a Minnie Mouse doll. There was a photograph of a young man's face, a pair of eyeglasses, a Chinese fan, and amid all these offerings there were votive candles and statues of the Virgin and the saints, all of this in gratitude for healing, or the hope of healing. When I looked more closely, I saw that THANKS was repeated over and over again in the alcove, stamped onto stones in the shapes of hearts or simple rectangles. I saw that the floor of the alcove was entirely paved with white stones that all said THANKS.

18

As I said, I had driven to Meridian a few weeks earlier. There were no hotels downtown, so I stayed on the outskirts on a highway lined with chain stores, chain restaurants, a profusion of choices so familiar they were almost invisible, like channels on cable. The downtown was a remnant of empty brick buildings, empty storefronts, a forlorn strip where one last shop displayed clothes in the colors of Valentine's Day. I was supposed to meet Mason in a park near where he said he lived, but when I arrived I didn't see him, so I sat in my car for a while. The once-staid houses around the park were dilapidated almost to the point of ruin, roofs falling in, doors and windows missing—a mattress in the street, scraps of aluminum awning, an old wheelchair, two velvet armchairs on a lawn. It was gray and damp as I got out of the car and wandered toward a statue of a man depicted in the heavy suit and waistcoat and walrus mustache of a merchant from after the Civil War. A sign announced that these "32 informally landscaped acres" were established in 1909 as "one of the South's premier streetcar pleasure parks" and contained "an 1890s Dentzel Carousel." I had never heard of a streetcar pleasure park or a Dentzel Carousel. Around the statue of the man, who was named I. A. Marks, were a few untended roses in a bed covered in dead leaves. When I went back to the parking lot, I saw Mason this time, smoking a cigarette beneath the roof of a bandshell with white wooden pillars, dwarfed by the branches of a tree that grew up beside it. He wore a black winter coat and a black knit cap and dark sweatpants. He didn't acknowledge me as I approached, and when I called out his name he just looked down at the ground, and for a moment I wasn't sure it was him, and yet I could feel even from that distance that it was. I stood at the foot of the bandshell and he looked down at me briefly, then turned his eyes to the distance. He asked me how Sonia was. He said he'd like to go visit Sonia one of these days in New Orleans, that he hadn't been down there in many years. He used to have a son there, he said, but the son lived now with his mother up north in Delaware. Heroin, he said, pronouncing it "hair-ine." He'd told me about that part of his life already, he said.

We were standing now at the bottom of the bandshell, and he pulled from his back pants pocket a rubber-banded stack of small pamphlets. I looked into his eyes and I wondered if he was high or if that was just how he appeared, as he told me about the religious faith described in the pamphlet. Inside were the usual admonitions:

IF YOU SHOULD DIE TODAY, WHERE WOULD YOU SPEND ETERNITY?

EVERY PERSON BORN INTO THIS WORLD INHERITED
A SINFUL NATURE.

THIS SINFUL NATURE PRODUCES ALL SORTS OF EVIL
DEEDS.

THERE IS NOTHING YOU CAN DO TO SAVE YOURSELF.

JUST BELIEVING INTELLECTUALLY THAT YOU ARE A
SINNER, THAT GOD LOVES YOU, AND THAT CHRIST DIED
FOR YOU IS NOT ENOUGH.

He licked his lips in an effort to contain his emotions—
sadness, anger, I couldn't tell because he concealed them. I
was trying to pinpoint who he reminded me of and it occurred to me that he reminded me of my stepbrother, who
was named James but who as an adult had started calling
himself Jamz. My stepbrother—like my half brother, like
my father—was no longer alive. He'd died of cancer, and before that he'd struggled with depression and alcoholism and
drug addiction. For many years I didn't see him. Toward the
end of his life, he became a bashful, frail person, and I saw
a similar frailty now in Mason, who spoke softly, with an
embarrassed deliberateness, and I thought of those stories
Marcus had told me about Mason and Kendrick as teen-
agers—the hip-hop and the BMX bikes, the action movies,
how they'd injured each other in fake fights simply because
they were so full of life. *A clown type*, Marcus had said. *A court
jester type.*

I asked Mason about those days now and he told me
that he was hit by a car when he was fourteen—"surgeries,
painkillers," he explained—and that was how he'd started
on "the wrong path." In high school, he said, there was a

white kid a grade ahead of him whose family knew Mason's mother and who would sometimes give her hand-me-down clothes. He remembered coming to school one day in one of the kid's T-shirts, which had a rock star's face on it, and when he saw the other boy, neither of them could "really handle it, it was awkward, you could feel something between us." The next time he saw the kid he was "stoned out my mind," and he got the other kid up against a cafeteria door and started punching his face, over and over, missing more than he connected, his fist pounding the steel, his knuckles bleeding. He said the ugliness he'd let out of himself that morning was what he started feeling most of the time after that. He dropped out of school. A few years later, he ended up living in New Orleans, drifting from place to place. New Orleans had always been a refuge, he said, an escape from the crowded house in Los Angeles that was "all women—my mother, three sisters, you couldn't get a minute to yourself there."

"My boy in the penitentiary," he said then, "he would sit with me every night last year and make me read the Bible with him. That's when things started to change for me. I saw that God loved me. He had my back, in spite of the guilt I carried about Kendrick. It was something I never got over. How I always felt it was my fault."

He said that his friend in prison had told him that the differences between people's faces were so small that if you measured them scientifically their faces would turn out to be almost the same. When his friend said this, he told me, his first thought was that he was talking about women. You were attracted to certain women based on tiny differences that made it hard to even talk to them because they seemed so important, but that wasn't what his friend meant. He said he'd missed his friend's point about faces at first because he'd always been so closed off from other people, putting up a front that appeared hard but was really just a blank. It was because shyness had always been a problem for him, he said, ever since he was a child. When he got older, he was so shy he preferred getting high to being with women. It was still that way, he admitted.

"I been this way a long time," he said. "Afraid to look into the eyes of other people. Afraid to look into my own eyes. Every person born in this world has a sinful nature, it says there in that paper I just gave you. Every person is the same that way."

I kept reaching for premature analogies, reminded again of my stepbrother, Jamz, whose depression, like the one Mason was describing now, came with a flipside of carelessness, even clownishness, and which made it easier for him to slip into oblivion. When I was young, he would buy me liquor, and my friends and I would sometimes get high with him in his bedroom until we got tired of it, and then we'd leave him by himself, living in our basement, having suffered a breakdown when he was away at college. One night I went down to the basement by myself—he'd asked me to come down—and I found him standing in front of the bathroom mirror, pouring rum into his throat straight from the bottle. He was naked—he needed me to see that for some reason, his naked body in the bathroom

light. Years later when he stopped drinking, stopped using drugs, he bought himself a collection of guns, and I
remember his displaying them for me one afternoon after
inviting me over to his apartment to see how much better
he was doing. We sat in his little kitchenette while he took
the guns one by one out of their leather case. There was a
revolver so large it was hard to believe it was real. He, of
course, knew what had happened to my father. I was young.
I didn't know how hard he'd been fighting all this time just
to be himself. I thought he might be about to shoot me for
being saner than he was.

Mason told me now that Kendrick had never been a serious heroin user, that he just dabbled. But that story he'd
told me about Athena Street, he said, was not true. Everyone
knew Athena Street was a place to score drugs. "He was saying that because of me," he said. "Even after all these years,
he's still keeping silent about that."

They'd had jobs for a while that summer of the murder,
he said, Mason at a Best Buy, Kendrick at a grocery store
called Save-A-Lot, but mostly when they were together they
liked to "act stupid, go to clubs, smoke weed," and it was
in this spirit that they went to meet some of their friends
that Friday on the West Bank, on Athena Street. He said it
was as if he and Kendrick had "almost switched roles" that
day, for Kendrick was usually the one in high spirits, the
one with money, and Mason was usually the one in trouble,
but now Kendrick was wearing Mason's old tracksuit, his
head shaved because he was "still tripping from his time in
jail. He couldn't get that feel off his skin, that dirt. That

was why he shaved his head like that. It was ten days, his first time locked up that long. I remember I picked him up that Friday after his court date. After they let him out, after Janelle made bail, he still had a court date. She had to be at work, so I went. It must have been strange for him, because I was driving him in his old car. He was riding with me in his old car, and I remember I took him to the barbershop and he end up getting his head shaved, I mean totally bald. I remember I paid for it because he was broke. I lent him some clothes. We just kept driving after that, over to the West Bank, until we run into Antoinette. When we was together, we thought everything was like a movie. I don't mean a serious movie, I mean a stupid movie, a stupid comedy, that kind of movie."

I asked him why he had Kendrick's old car.

"He gave it to you?" I asked.

"He didn't need a car. He could always use Janelle's car if he had to. He was like that, though—he was generous with people. That's why he kept going back and forth with Janelle and Desiree, Janelle and Desiree, because he was too soft-hearted to break up with either of them. That's why he gave me the car. He knew I was struggling with some things, so he wanted to do me a kindness. He had friends all over the place, friends everywhere. It came natural to him—friends, girls—we were almost opposites that way."

We had stopped walking and were standing now in front of the statue of I. A. Marks, Mason's black cap pushed down a little too far on his forehead as he bowed his head and lit a cigarette. It was understood by now, I gathered, that what

had happened on Athena Street that Friday was what set in
motion the murder of Damien Martin three days later. It
occurred to me that Mason might have been involved in the
murder in precisely the way that Kendrick had been accused
of being involved, but I didn't feel the danger I thought I
should feel, or rather the sense of danger was mixed with an
unwanted pity for us both, a pity that reminded me again of
how I'd felt that afternoon in my stepbrother's kitchenette
when he showed me his guns. I asked Mason if he'd lost
money the day Damien Martin was killed, and he looked at
me with less surprise than I expected, which made me pity
us even more. He and Kendrick and Antoinette were going
to buy fifty dollars' worth of heroin that Friday, he said. It
was what you did when you quit or got fired from your job
at Best Buy or the grocery store, you pooled some money
together and "hustled a little." They went with Antoinette
to pawn a ring at the Cash America, he said, but when
they got to the pawnshop she realized she'd forgotten her
ID, so Kendrick let her borrow his. She fronted Kendrick
some money, because he had helped her with the ID. He
said that he heard later that Antoinette had told the police
she'd heard cabinets slamming when the murder happened
the next Monday. "Cabinets slamming," he said. "You ever
heard a gunshot, you know it don't sound like no cabinets
slamming. She's covering up. Fifty dollars. You asked if I
lost money, that's how much money we lost that day. Fifty
dollars. It looks different now because of what ended up
happening—a dead body, my cousin in prison his whole life.
This little nothing deal turning into something like that."

He said that they gave the money from the pawnshop to a friend who was supposed to buy drugs, but that she didn't come back from Texas that weekend. She was the mother of Damien Martin's daughters, Jodi Batiste. She and Damien had lived next door to Antoinette and Lawrence until they broke up and Jodi moved to Metairie, while Damien stayed on Athena Street. Years later, he said, he'd heard that Jodi Batiste ended up going to prison for several years on a drug charge. Lawrence was, of course, in prison, Kendrick was in prison, Damien was dead. The only other person involved in the story besides him—Antoinette—was free, he said, because she'd "lied."

His voice had gone from stern to neutral then almost inaudible. He had turned away, his eyes closed in shame, and I noticed for the first time a birthmark on the back of his cheek, like a smear of ash on his skin. He said that the money wasn't even what was on Kendrick's mind when he called him that Monday, the morning of the murder. All Kendrick had wanted, he said, was a ride to Desiree's apartment in Slidell. Janelle was at work all that day. He had his chance to leave her for Desiree while she was away, but he'd given his car to Mason.

"When he called that morning, I knew by then that something had gone wrong. I remember I just said to forget it. You thinking about Desiree? I had seen Lawrence the night before, you understand? We was both sick out our minds. Lawrence, he been shot in the leg just a few weeks before this. We wasn't straight, neither of us, we needed to get high. Lawrence must have been crazy that morning.

I said to Kendrick I'd call him later. He's thinking about Desiree. He's probably waiting for me that whole day in Janelle's trailer, waiting for me to call him back."

"You knew what had happened."

"I ain't said I knew what happened. I just knew I wasn't calling no one. I already told you about the kind of problems I had. It was my turn to help out Kendrick, but by the time he called, I was sick—dope-sick and scared out my mind— and I'd seen Lawrence the night before. I already sensed there was a problem."

"Did you drive over there that morning?"

"Drive where?"

"To Athena Street."

"No."

"Because that would explain some things."

"Like I said, I had seen Lawrence the night before. It ain't no need to drive over there."

"Maybe you did it anyway, though."

"I needed to get high. That was all I cared about. When I found out later, that's when I knew what happened. Before that, I didn't know and I didn't want to know."

Across from the bandshell, there was a museum dedicated to the country music star Jimmie Rodgers, who'd been born in Meridian. Mason said he needed to use the bathroom, but when he tried the front door it was locked— the museum was closed that day—so he changed his mind, saying he wanted to make a phone call, he needed some privacy for a minute, and he walked behind the building. There were two antique train cars there, a black engine and

a red caboose. I stood waiting for a while, then decided I
didn't want to be there when he first came back. I didn't
know how much of what he'd just said was true, but if he'd
been present during the murder, I doubted he would have
agreed to meet with me in the first place. Then I thought of
a man I'd met at Angola, who, like Kendrick, had told me
he was innocent. They were the only two inmates I'd met
who said that. It turned out that the other man wasn't really
innocent. He had been nineteen when he was left alone to
babysit his infant stepson, whom he'd loved, and it was that
love that made it impossible for him to believe that he could
have lost his temper and accidentally shaken the baby to
death. He wasn't exactly lying to me when he said he hadn't
done this. He was reporting what he believed to be true.

I walked over to the Dentzel Carousel, which was across
a large field. It was also closed that day, perhaps because it
was winter, but when I got near enough to its wooden enclosure I could see through the window glare the beautifully
painted animals—horses, a lion, a deer, a giraffe, a tiger—
standing still on their brass poles. I imagined Damien
Martin opening his apartment door, the room behind him
dark from the blackout curtains pulled up close against the
windows. I imagined him seeing Lawrence Jeffries standing
there with sweat on his face, denim shorts over the gauze
wrapped around his leg where the bullet wound was. I
couldn't tell if he was standing there by himself or standing
there with Mason—all I could see was Lawrence. *Cabinets
slamming. You ever heard a gunshot, you know it don't sound like no
cabinets slamming.* I thought of my stepbrother, who'd died

of cancer, my half brother, who had stopped talking to me, and I thought of how none of those occurrences, like the murder of my father, had ever seemed truly connected to me or even possible. My detachment from them seemed to have led me all the way to this empty park with Mason in his black clothes and hat, coming back now from behind the museum, a blankness in his eyes, which were all pupil. It was clear he couldn't talk much longer, or perhaps just that I couldn't. His eyes locked on mine now in a tearful haze of need that somehow spoke of the dishonor he felt about everything he'd just told me. Heroin. *Hair-ine.* I thanked him for talking to me and told him I would call him later if he wanted. We gave each other a loose hug, his coat musty with the smell of his hair and his cigarettes. These moments as they're described in books are seldom as they are—the jostle and rush of separation, the confusion and disappointment, the sense of misunderstanding and resentment, violation and gratitude. I thanked him again, and he nodded faintly, moving away. It wasn't hard to imagine that he lived there in that park.

19

I woke up early the next morning in my hotel room, not knowing at first where I was. I could see the TV's black screen, the empty carton of food, the bottle on the nightstand, the plastic cups. I had tried to call Mason the evening before but I somehow knew that I wouldn't reach him and that he wouldn't call me back. I didn't want to talk to him anyway. I didn't want to talk to anyone—I had known days ago that I would feel this way, before I'd even left for Meridian.

When I couldn't get back to sleep, I put on some clothes and went down to the lobby to get some coffee from the breakfast area. The woman setting out food there saw me without seeing me, her uniform of polo shirt and name tag designed to make her, too, almost invisible. I had a copy of the local newspaper, which I was going to use as a shield from conversation with other guests, and perhaps she sensed this. The TV news was on. I hadn't called home last night to Sarah. I'd begun thinking that freedom could

be a kind of wound, something we couldn't tolerate without
something equally great to assuage it, which I knew had to
be love, but the word *love* sounded absurd to me. I knew that
one way to make it less absurd would be to simply say hello
to the other people in the breakfast area and so I made the
effort to do so. There was a group of soldiers in camouflage fatigues eating waffles from the machine. There was
an elderly couple in T-shirts and shorts, and when I greeted
them, unlike the soldiers, they wanted to keep talking, but
I just wanted to be by myself, so I let it fade. I understood
that without the soldiers I would not have had all the things
I had and yet I feared the American flag every time I saw
it. The mayor of Flint, Michigan, had just declared a state
of emergency because there was lead in the city's water. I
was at a La Quinta Inn in Meridian, Mississippi, watching this on TV. I remembered Mason coming out from
behind the museum in the park yesterday, and then I remembered him standing there smoking beneath the white
bandshell when I first saw him from across the parking lot.
After we'd said goodbye, I drove a few miles out of town to
the East Mississippi Correctional Facility, the prison he'd
done his time in, a complex of cinder-block buildings with
blue aluminum roofs and no windows, surrounded by wire.
Except for the wire, it looked like a factory farm for raising
poultry. There were corrections officers in the parking lots
on the way to their shifts, all of them younger than Mason,
young black men and women in dark blue uniforms, who
must have known many of the people they were being paid
to guard.

It made little sense that Lawrence Jeffries would murder his own next-door neighbor. But it made more sense than Kendrick doing it with him. It at least made some sense that Lawrence would do it by himself, out of desperation—by himself, or maybe with Mason.

I went back up to my room to take a shower, trying not to let my mind keep wandering, because I was still having spells of dizziness. When I washed my face, I took care to plant my feet and stand directly facing the blast, running my fingers over my eyebrows several times to make sure no water or soap got into my eyes once I opened them. I saw the painted animals on the Dentzel Carousel back in the park. I imagined Mason standing there with me like a tour guide, both of us crouching and peering through the glass. I shampooed my hair—rinsing it out with my back to the water, then trying to turn around with my eyes still closed to wash the shampoo from my face—but I lost all sense of where I was. The room spun, causing me to stagger, my feet sliding, eyes stinging with soap now, everything a blur. I touched the wall with one hand and the room seemed to tip to the other side and I fell the other way. I hit my shin hard against the edge of the tub and found myself on my back, the water pouring over me. The room was turning in slow diagonals end over end. I had no idea what had just happened. My shin was a pink smear of blood and water and wet hair. My naked body looked sexless and frail. I didn't know if I'd done harm to myself or was just imagining all of this. When I came back into the moment, I managed to kneel for a few seconds, then get up, bending over with my hands on the edge of the tub, then finally standing. I let the water wash over me long after I was clean. When I turned it off and dried myself, I had to sit on the toilet for a long time with a towel pressed to my shin to stop the bleeding. Then I hobbled over to the phone in the next room and called down to the front desk to have them send up some bandages.

The book I'd been reading last night, James Baldwin's *Notes of a Native Son*, was splayed open on the foot of the king-size bed. I picked it up and glanced at a random passage:

> In America, though, life seems to move faster than anywhere else on the globe and each generation is promised more than it will get; which creates, in each generation, a furious, bewildered rage, the rage of people who can't find solid ground beneath their feet.

I saw now that the night of the murder had started out for Kendrick much less seriously than I'd ever understood. He was just going to drive from Janelle's to Desiree's, knowing he would have to come back later that night to return Janelle's car. He stopped on the way at Athena Street to see what was happening, perhaps wondering where his cousin Mason was, why no one had called him all day, and perhaps also to pick up his share of the heroin, so he could bring it to Desiree's apartment in Slidell, either to use it or hide it there, or both. I remembered that on my way back from the East Mississippi Correctional Facility yesterday I had stopped for gas, and as I was standing at the

pump, I'd thought about buying some beer, but instead I'd
ended up buying whiskey. I remembered that the moment
I saw the bottle behind the cash register I knew I would
drink too much. There was a rapper named Big K.R.I.T.
who was from Meridian and whose name meant "King
Remembered in Time." Kendrick's last name of course
was King. I remembered thinking late that night that this
was significant, making a note of it, half the bottle gone, a
writer with too much time on his hands, my laptop open
so I could browse the Internet at the same time I watched
the TV.

The downtown of Meridian had been practically abandoned, as I said, but the restaurant where I went for lunch
that afternoon was still popular—it was the oldest restaurant in Mississippi, according to its sign. When I finished
eating, I took a walk and experienced a strange gratifica-
tion in the way my gouged shin was painlessly buffered by
the bandages between it and my pants leg. I noticed this
time that some of the old brick buildings in Meridian had
faded advertisements painted on their sides, the names of
banks, accounting firms, insurance agents, merchants, and I
saw that some of the names, like the name of the restaurant
I'd eaten in, Weidmann's, were Jewish or at least probably
Jewish. I thought of the occasional references, never flat-
tering, to Jewish merchants in W. E. B. Du Bois's account
of the post–Civil War South in *The Souls of Black Folk* and

how these references made me slightly tense. I thought of
the antagonistic relationships between Jews and blacks that
Baldwin described in his essay "The Harlem Ghetto" in
Notes of a Native Son. I'm mentioning all this because there
was a storefront a few blocks down from Weidmann's with
a newly painted orange façade and a brown sign that said
HOUSE OF ISRAEL HEBREW CULTURE CENTER, which
would not have looked out of place in Brooklyn but which
surprised me here. I wondered who the proprietors were, if
they were some vestige of that post–Civil War Jewish community or, less likely, a group of Jews who had settled here
in order to start a small congregation where property was
cheap. I was thinking all this as I walked back to the orange building, having decided to take a picture of it with
my phone. Another possibility occurred to me, just as I was
taking the picture, which was that it was a Black Hebrew
Israelite temple, and as I was having this thought, a black
man, who must have seen me as I went through these hesi-
tations, came up and introduced himself. I'd seen him just
before this through the window of a shop, where he was
working with a belt sander, a surgical mask over his face.
He had come out of the shop now to say hello. He said
he was the rabbi of this congregation. He asked if I was
"Charles," and I said no, and he explained that Charles was
someone who was planning on stopping by that afternoon.
I said I hoped he didn't mind that I was taking a picture of
his building and he said no, of course not, and I told him
then I was Jewish, that that was why I'd wanted to take the

picture. He said he was Jewish, too. We were both smiling now, though I wasn't even sure why. I asked him how long he'd been a rabbi there. He said he'd been there only a few years but that he'd been Jewish forever.

He invited me in. The temple was a dark space with a few pews and an altar and an ark behind it for the Torah. I thought of the religious pamphlet Mason had given me yesterday, with its bold-faced admonitions, for the rabbi now offered me several photocopied articles to read: "The Truth About Christmas," "The Truth About Easter," "New Year According to God." They turned out to be calmly argued essays about the pagan provenance of certain Christian rituals. He explained now that his religion believed in Christ as the savior but that its liturgy was Jewish. They celebrated the Sabbath on Saturday, not Sunday; they kept kosher; they held a seder during Passover, and even lived in tents during the feast of Sukkot. I realized that if I had met him even a few years ago I might have hesitated to take him seriously before he had a chance to tell me any of this. *Tikkun olam* is the Hebrew phrase that means "repairing the world." In the Jewish mystical tradition, the ten vessels that contained the emanation of God's light, the *sephirot*, could not withstand the pressure and exploded. I told him about this myth now because, I said, it had meant more to me in my life than the Judaism I'd grown up with. Our task on earth, according to this myth, was to repair the shattered vessels, the shattered world, which meant that first of all we had to pay careful attention to it. I told him then about why I was in Meridian in the first place—about the passion play I'd seen at Angola, about Kendrick, about how I hadn't been able to stop thinking about him and others like him in the last two years. He asked me what I thought of all the talk lately about prison, about mass incarceration, and I came up against some knowledge I'd only recently acquired, which was that there were limits to how comfortably I could talk about incarceration with someone who had grown up with it as a familiar threat, or a stigma, or a reasonable possibility, simply because of the color of his skin. There was no tension between us. I told him what I thought and he just nodded, taking in what I had to say. Then he gave me something to read, a passage from Isaiah:

> *But this is a people robbed and*
> *   plundered;*
> *All of them are snared in holes,*
> *And they are hidden in prison*
> *   houses;*
> *They are for prey, and no one*
> *   delivers;*
> *For plunder, and no one says,*
> *   "Restore!"*
> *Who among you will give ear to*
> *   this?*
> *Who will listen and hear for the*
> *   time to come?*
> *Who gave Jacob for plunder, and*
> *   Israel to the robbers?*
> *Was it not the Lord,*

He against whom we have sinned?
For they would not walk in His
   ways,
Nor were they obedient to His law.
Therefore He has poured on him
   the Fury of His anger
And the strength of battle;
It has set him on fire all around,
Yet he did not know;
And it burned him,
Yet he did not take it to heart.

I didn't know how to respond to this. The way it seemed to apportion blame didn't make sense to me, but though I objected to it, it troubled me more and more the longer I considered it. I realized that it meant something to him that it couldn't mean to me. I didn't say this, but instead told him about how I wasn't scared of Mason yesterday when he'd given me his version of what had happened to Damien Martin. It had occurred to me that Mason might have been involved in the murder himself, I said, but it hadn't felt that way, and I'd just kept thinking about how Mason reminded me of my stepbrother, with whom he shared a similar bashfulness. I said that I tended to see pattern and coincidence and analogy, but that I didn't trust the urge to find significance or deeper meaning in these correspondences, or in my perceptions in general. But in spite of that, I said, the God

in the book of Isaiah retained a certain power over me, beyond my understanding.

He nodded, though all I'd really said was that I didn't
understand how the passage from Isaiah applied to what I'd
seen at Angola.

"*Tikkun olam,*" he said. "I never heard of that before."

"It's something I read somewhere. It doesn't mean I put
it into practice."

"I see it, though."

"Vengeance. I see that, too," I said. "Some sort of general principle. Justified or not. God as a wave of violence."

We smiled at each other again. There was still no tension between us. He said there were a few ex-convicts he
knew here in Meridian that he could put me in touch with if
I wanted to talk to them. One of them ran a car wash just up
the street, where he tried to help out other men who'd been
in prison or had a hard time in other ways. Another one
ran a barbecue restaurant on the way back toward my hotel. He said the restaurant was supposed to be pretty good,
but he'd never tried it—it wasn't kosher. We smiled at that,
too. He told me he had grown up in New Orleans. Many
years ago, he said, he had played in a reggae band at a club
on Frenchmen Street. I told him that my friend Deborah,
the photographer who had brought me to Angola, lived on
Frenchmen Street. I told him our whole story—how our
parents had both been murdered in the same city, how we
lived just two blocks away from each other now, how you

could see my roof from her roof. Fate, coincidence—I said I could see the uncanniness of it, but again I resisted the idea of meaning. *There's a divinity that shapes our ends, rough-hew them how we will*, wrote Shakespeare, and though the line sounded persuasive, I also knew that it was spoken by Hamlet, who got everything wrong.

The walk to the car wash took me out of the city center in just a few blocks, past a derelict building with the name Wyckoff painted on it in fading green letters, then on to a strip of warehouses, a transmission shop, a run-down bar with a portable toilet outside. It was another gray day and the colors of the litter on the sides of the road stood out with a hallucinatory glow—red, yellow, blue—beneath the black limbs of the trees. The car wash was in a squat building made of orange cinder blocks, a former garage with no cars out in front of it. I saw Mason standing there. He was in the empty lot with two other men, their heads bowed, talking and smoking cigarettes. He wore the same black clothes and jacket and cap he'd worn yesterday. When I walked up to say hello, it took us a moment to realize that we were both going to pretend that I hadn't tried to call him last night and that he hadn't avoided calling me back. He was looking down at his knuckles while rubbing them slowly with the other hand. His face, with its pencil mustache, was like a face you'd see in photographs of jazz musicians from the 1940s, but perhaps more accurately it revealed those photographs to be distortions, making their subjects less ordinary than they actually were. I asked him if we could talk for a few more minutes and he shook his head faintly, his eyes distant.

"It was nothing I could do to help Kendrick," he said.

I asked him what he meant, and he explained that he had left town right after the murder, several days before Kendrick's arrest. By then, he said, Lawrence and Antoinette had put together their story.

"They would have gone hard on someone like Antoinette," he said. "They would have told her they're gonna put her in jail, take away her child. It's a lot of pressure they can put on a female. She had to make a choice. Like I said, I had left town. Kendrick was still there. At first, she tried to say that Kendrick was the one who killed Damien. Lawrence tried to say it was Kendrick who killed Damien. Eventually, everyone said what they had to say. Everyone except Kendrick."

"They tried to say that he drove there in his car that morning," I said.

"They said a lot of things."

"Was it you who drove his car there?"

He stayed silent.

"They just thought that up themselves?" I asked.

"Even if I drove it, I wouldn't tell you, right?"

The other two men had been standing in silence, pretending I wasn't there. Mason brought his lips in tight, as if about to spit.

"I'll never get over it," he said. "Why you think I was talking to you yesterday, telling you all those things?"

It was because, I realized after I thought about it for a while, he was innocent too. Innocent, but in the narrowest way. Innocent, in that he had driven the car there to see what was happening, but had left before the murder, having continued on elsewhere to look for the drugs he needed but hadn't himself killed for.

20

LAGARDE: Mr. King, uh, is it not in fact true that, oh, maybe twenty minutes ago, sometime before 6:00 p.m. on this date, you called the detective bureau, looking for me?

KING: Yes.

LAGARDE: Okay, and what caused you to do that?

KING: Well, because my mother had called me and told me that two detectives had come by the house. She said you gave her your card, so I called you right away.

LAGARDE: And so, after a brief conversation, we came back here into this interview room.

KING: Yes, sir.

LAGARDE: And I said that this was in regard to Damien Martin, who had been murdered the week before.

KING: Yes.

LAGARDE: And I asked you if you knew him.

KING. Yes.

LAGARDE: And you indicated that you did know him.

KING: Yes.

LAGARDE: And I asked you if you had been around the building at all on the day of the murder, in the morning hours, in particular, on the day in question. If, you know, you could account for your whereabouts, during those morning hours. And what did you say?

KING: No, I wasn't there during the morning hours.

LAGARDE. Okay. That's right. You indicated that you were not there in the morning hours.

KING: That's right.

LAGARDE: And when you first told me that, only then did I start filling out this form I'm showing you now, entitled "Jefferson Parish Sheriff's Office Rights of Arrestee or Suspect."

KING: Yes. That's correct.

The photographs are still on the table—the pictures of Damien's dead body, the pictures of the young black men in their white T-shirts, Lawrence's face among the others, his eyes now a threat, as if he could have somehow known when the picture was taken that it would end up here. In the interrogation room, there's a glass transom above the closed door, a coat hook on the door itself, the door painted white, the knob made of silver steel with an unlocked bolt above it made of the same silver metal. Right at the edge of the door frame is an unusually narrow light switch that is made of the same silver metal. Kendrick has been seeing these things for so long in the even fluorescent light without really looking at them that it's as if the objects now have sight and are watching him. They have formed into a pattern, like spectators in the bleachers of a sparsely attended game. There's a gruesome picture of Damien, his head resting on a blood-soaked cloth laid atop a plastic sheet, a stream of blood issuing from his nostrils, his eyes blurry slits, maroon-colored spatters on his cheeks and nose. There are more than a dozen close-ups of the bullet wounds to his forehead, temple, and ear, small round holes seeping with blood as dark and viscous as oil. Lagarde has his hand on the table, three of his finger-tips touching the edge of the stack of photographs, his short sleeves revealing the unpleasant paleness of his bare fore-arms, which have almost no hair on them. There's some-thing prim about the way he sits, as if taking satisfaction in his ability to confront this ugliness, a boyish pathos in the little half-moon scar beneath his left eye. This sense of decency makes Kendrick more and more afraid the longer they stay here. The floor is tiled with gray linoleum squares textured with darker gray flecks to make it hard to tell how dirty it is. He looks at the wall near his shoulder, which is painted white and has an electrical conduit running up its center from the floor to the ceiling.

"How many times do you think he was shot, to look like that?" Lagarde asks.

The other detective comes in with two cans of Coke, but Kendrick doesn't open his. He sees his hands on the table in the gray light, his bare calves beneath his black soccer shorts, his ankles tapering down into white Adidas shell-toe shoes. He feels shiny and exposed, as Lagarde drinks from his can of soda, not looking at Kendrick but at the manila folder on his side of the desk, the other detective leaving now.

"What happened with this arrest you had a few weeks back?" Lagarde finally asks, still not looking up.

"What arrest?"

"This arrest in Orleans Parish. It looks like you had a court appearance just a week ago. Ten days ago."

"I spent some time in Orleans. Ten days."

"In jail."

"Yes."

"So you know what this process consists of, then."

Kendrick looks at him. "What process?"

"You've been arrested before. And so you know that once someone's under arrest, the next thing would be for them to be transferred to lockup to await arraignment. Like now, because it's already late, you'd end up spending the night there. And after that, the likely outcome is that you'd stay in lockup until trial. Either that or you'd need to make bail."

"What is this?"

Lagarde places the manila folder on top of the stack of crime-scene photographs. It's just the folders and the mug shots now, Lawrence's face an angry blur among the other angry blurs.

"We know you were there that morning," Lagarde says.

"What?"

"We know you were on Athena Street that morning to buy drugs. Actually, we know you were there in the apartment when the murder happened. We've known that for a while now."

"What do you mean?"

"I mean, we know you were in the apartment when Damien Martin was killed."

The smudge marks on the white door seem to faintly pulsate for a moment. The coat hook and the doorknob and the light switch no longer seem watchful but have gone back to being simple objects. They're no longer watchful because there's no longer anything distinctive about Kendrick to see. He feels another surge of panic and guilt that is the feeling of being in jail, then there's an absurd moment when he keeps saying *What?* and Lagarde keeps saying *We know you were there* and it goes back and forth like that until finally Lagarde says, *Stop saying "what."*

He remembers the picture of Damien Martin sprawled dead on the floor in the kitchen, lying beside a bucket of joint compound and a mop in a plastic pail. His shirt is rolled up to his rib cage and his face rests in a pool of purple-and-red blood that stretches all the way down the length of his arm to his fingertips. When Kendrick first saw it, he knew that Lagarde knew that he recognized the linoleum of the floor, the yellow of the dishwasher, even the dark clothes Damien was wearing, and though he knew he hadn't been there, he also felt that in some way he had. It was Damien on the floor, Damien with bullet holes in his face, and you couldn't look at a picture like that of someone you knew without internalizing its obscenity—it was as if by not being there you had somehow allowed it to happen; it spoke to some general wrong inside you. There's a terrible understanding now that Lagarde has been polite this whole time not because he's polite but because he's so completely comfortable with the idea that Kendrick was there, that Lagarde has thought this all along. Similarly, he understands now that Lagarde's blandness is no indication of who he is but is just a physical accident, what he happens to look like. Everything up to this point between them has been a pretense that Kendrick has failed to examine closely enough, Lagarde waiting patiently for him to say as many stupid things as he has—*Damien and Jodi has a baby, a little girl, and I wanted to see this little girl, 'cause my little girl is . . . like a few months older*—so that everything he says now will sound just as untruthful.

"I don't know what you're talking about," Kendrick says now.

"We have two witnesses who know you were there. We already know what happened. Why it happened. What I find hard to believe, though, is that you were the one who shot Damien. You and not your friend Lawrence. That doesn't seem right to me."

"I don't know what you mean."

"I think your friend Lawrence was the shooter, not you, is what I'm trying to say."

"He's not my friend."

"We have two witnesses who say you were the shooter. Let's talk about that, not about who your friends are."

21

I would dream of what happened next in that interrogation room. *Fill in the gaps, make it sound more convincing,* Kendrick had said Lagarde had told him when he took the stand at his trial. I would dream of the absurdities acted out in that little room, Lagarde offering suggestions about what really happened, getting out of his chair to work out the angle of Kendrick's sight line, the position of Lawrence and Damien outside the kitchen when the first shot was fired, the second shot, the third. *Did he hold up his hands then? Like this or like that? Which way did he fall?* I would dream of the odd momentum that accrued as they worked out the details of this fiction, Kendrick spurred on partly because these scenarios focused on Lawrence, not on him—he was not the shooter, he was cooperating, he was saying what Lagarde needed him to say in order to get out of this room, knowing that since it was all lies it would all be easy to disprove later. They rehearsed it over and over, smoothing out the edges and repeating it in its polished form, so that Kendrick's voice, when they

made the second tape, was remarkably calm and deliberate, just as it had been on the first tape, even though his
very first statement now was a lie: *King: I drove to Athena Street
about 11:00 that morning. Lagarde: What were you driving? King: In a
Mazda. A Mazda Protégé.* I would dream all of this, and then
I would dream of Kendrick in the dorm at Angola, walking
to the showers in that vast space that seemed submerged
underwater, separate from the earth, or of him lying in his
bunk bed reading—Machiavelli, Leonardo, the Bible—the
cuffs of his jeans rolled up, one bare foot on the ground, the
other leg extended. The word *dream* is not quite accurate, for
I wasn't fully asleep when I pictured these scenes, or when
they played out for me against my will as I lay in the darkness, awake enough to know that the playacting I imagined was too clownish—Lagarde gesturing and lunging,
Kendrick sitting there with his hands improbably shackled
behind his chair—but every time I tried to fall fully asleep,
I would be back inside the dark farce. Whatever nightmare
was offered by that day's news—the ice caps melting, the
seas rising—would somehow find its way into the farce, no
matter how irrelevant or disconnected, for that was the cir-
cuitry of my mind.

No more Internet, no more iPhone, no more smoking,
drinking, marijuana. I had tried to enforce these rules for
myself over the last few months but had found it difficult to
sit still inside my restlessness, even when I was with other
people, even in conversation. Everything in comparison
to Kendrick's story and its ramifications seemed half-real.
When I read a book, after a few pages I would give in to

the overwhelming urge to sleep. The phone would be in the other room but I would still feel the pulse of its vibration running from my back pocket down my thigh. No one was calling, no one was texting. The boredom and restlessness of my free life, like the dizziness and disorientation, would abate for periods of time but never went away.

Almost ten years ago, I went to visit the garage where my father was murdered, because I knew that if you didn't face that kind of trauma it would always be waiting for you, camouflaged as something else, and I wanted to try to face it. *At the second underground level*, I wrote in my book, *I got out of the elevator alone. I pushed open the stairwell door and went inside . . . The stairwell was not wide enough for two people to stand in side by side. It was very cold that day, and the narrow space reeked of mildew and dust, as if the door had not been opened in a very long time. I knelt down on the first step—I knew I would do this and now I was doing it almost as a formality. The step was so solid that I felt an immediate pain in my knees and shins. I was shaking. My father would have been shaking, forty years old, a young man, not much older than I was that day. It was a tiny cement box in which to be executed. Forty minutes later, the dust was still in my mouth and my nose.*

I had thought that going there would make me a different person, as I'd told Janelle in Houston, but as I'd also told her, the strength I'd gained from going there came and went in unpredictable ways. I remember now going to school on the Monday after my father's murder, and because my teacher wasn't sure how to handle it, she asked me if I was okay. The class was already seated and it was from my desk near the back that I announced, as if bragging, perhaps even smiling, that "my dad got killed." I had thought I would be able to bluff my way through the incomprehensible event by pretending everything was fine, but my teacher looked at me like I was alien. You have to live, you have to pretend you're normal, but this means you end up facing your abnormality piecemeal, over the course of years, even over the course of a lifetime—every time you think you've faced it, you've only faced some of it. I've lived on two planes ever since my father's murder. It's made me different from other people, and I've tried to keep that sense of difference from becoming a sense of grandiosity or simple neurosis, but I haven't always succeeded. My friend Chris, a painter, used to have a note pinned up on his studio wall: *Give everything. Give it now.* After four books, more than twenty years of writing, I found myself, in the face of what Kendrick had gone through, asking, *Give what? Give it to whom?*

Several months after I met Mason in Meridian, I went for the first time to a sensory-deprivation tank, which was less dramatic than I'd thought it would be, though I hadn't expected it to be very dramatic anyway—it was simply a way to stop thinking so much. You take a shower in an ordinary bathroom, then you step into the tank, a white plastic box whose opened hatch is black, the chamber inside totally dark except for a faint green light at the back. You wear earplugs made of red putty, which I put in as I crouched there in the shallow salt water, having closed the door. Then I turned off the faint green light. I lay back thinking there wasn't enough water, but there was, I was able to float easily, and after that, there was nothing to do but wonder if I was maximizing the experience—if my posture was right, if I was better off closing my eyes or leaving them open, if enough of my head was submerged. This lasted several minutes— I knew it was stupid but didn't try to resist it. Eventually I moved past these ruminations and entered more deeply into the tank. The tiny space, hardly bigger than a coffin, became a black firmament above me, tinged by a faint green glow. When I put my arms at my side, I didn't hear my heart beating. All I heard was my own breathing—silence, then breathing, silence, then breathing. When I occasionally drifted, touching one of the sides of the tank, I found that I could bounce a little and spin and that in that whirling I lost my sense of space, that the tank felt far bigger than it was, an ocean at night, but that rather than feeling tiny and helpless I felt bigger and unbound. Sometimes I would lie there like a dead man, my mouth agape, arms limp, wallowing in passivity. At other times, I extended my arms above my head, reaching as high as I could, so that my face was almost underwater, just my eyes, nose, and mouth above the surface, and all I could hear then was the beating of my heart—no more breathing, just the heart's steady thud. You realize that the heart is at the center of the body, that the body is its servant—the arms and legs and head—all of it is for the heart, not for the brain. I could see a vision of my heart, a pistoned engine pumping in the darkness, and I thought of those Catholic images of the Sacred Heart, the thick muscle giving forth flames, bound by a crown of thorns, sometimes pierced with a sword. I don't want to make it sound more meaningful than it was. It was just an hour of peace that I didn't want to stop. The hour's end is signaled by the switching on of the jets, like a hot tub's. My whole head was tingling, overcome by a virulent enthusiasm that reminded me of how I felt after the first time I went skydiving. I turned on the light and opened the hatch and stepped back into the room like Jonah coming out of his whale.

22

Pardon and Parole Board
P.O. Box 94304—Capitol Station
Baton Rouge, LA 70804-94304

March 16, 2016

Dear Board,

Out of the belly of Sheol I cried. The waters surrounded me, even to my soul; the deep closed around me; weeds were wrapped around my head. I went down to the moorings of the mountains. The earth with its bars closed behind me forever.

I'm writing on behalf of Kendrick King (383660), whom I met three years ago when I was a guest at Angola prison. I was there working on a project with a photographer, who, like me, had a parent who was murdered many years ago. I don't know if she'd agree with what I've come to think since then. I almost certainly have different feelings

about the punishment of crime than you do, and
this is probably because I was so young—six—when
my father was murdered. When I was maybe ten or
twelve, I used to lie awake entertaining revenge fantasies about the man who had ordered the murder.
Around the same time I slept with a lacrosse stick
next to my bed, because I had nightmares and was
afraid of being attacked in my sleep. My room, after
my mother remarried, was in the basement of my
stepfather's house, and the windows of that room
gave out onto the backyard, which was adjacent to
a public golf course, which was adjacent to a main
road that became a highway into the mountains.
There was a burglar alarm system in my stepfather's
house that consisted of a single brass wire running
down the center of each window that would sound
an alarm if broken, but the wire seemed only to emphasize how easy it would be to break the glass. It
was not hard for me to imagine someone making his
way off the road that connected to the highway and
then walking across the golf course to my windows.
I would picture him watching me, invisible in the
darkness outside my room. One night my mother
came down because I sometimes screamed when I
had nightmares, and I almost hit her with the lacrosse stick. It terrified both of us. It embarrasses
me to remember it now. My point is that I used to
gratify myself on such nights by imagining the man
who had ordered my father's murder in a prison cell,

a cartoon of an old convict with a graying pompa-
dour in an old-fashioned gray prison workshirt and
pants, very unlike the way I'd seen him pictured
in photos, dressed in a suit and tie. I knew almost
nothing about him. In my childish imagination, he
had simply come to embody the danger we'd fled,
which had erased everything about our previous
lives, an erasure made literal by the armed police-
men waiting behind the wooden fence at the side of
our house in case someone came to kill my mother.
In these waking dreams, I would confront the man
in his jail cell and say what, do what?—I can't remember now. I assailed him with hate in some way
through the bars of his cell, which even as a ten- or
twelve-year-old boy I knew was preposterous. You
can see how futile and empty such fantasies came
to seem after a short while, even for such a young
boy. It did no good to have the man in a cage and to
shout my hatred at him. It had nothing to do with
what had happened. I had a father who was murdered, and while I believe that something could
have been done to prevent it, I don't believe that
anything could have been done to rectify it. It was
beyond rectifying.

I believe that there are people who are so dangerous to others that they should be kept from
carrying out further harm. But most people in
prison are there not for the public's safety but out

of vengeance, or hatred, or because if they were
let out we would have to help them. After twelve
years in prison, Kendrick King, like most people,
has changed so much that it's as though a different
person is now serving his time. I'm not even talking about the fact that I think he's innocent. His
daughter's name is Aysha—she's a teenager now,
reminiscent of Kendrick in many ways. The last
time I saw her, she had a new phone, and when she
entered me into her contacts she used emojis instead of letters, renaming me in this way. When she
showed me what she'd done, it was like confronting
an image of myself at her age, a vision of my own
former mockery and disdain, the alienation that
comes with growing up fatherless. What I'm asking you is to imagine putting someone like Aysha
in prison. I have a good life now—a home, a wife I
love, money—but I know that much of that is luck,
redounding to my surface, even to the color of my
skin, which in this time and place is called "white."
I'm writing this letter because I know Kendrick
won't write to you himself. He hasn't given up—he
has always had some vague idea or other of how he
might get free, but it's as if his hope is too fragile to
sustain any effort to take real action. I know this
letter is unlikely to do any good. I feel like Jonah,
vomited out of the whale and finally delivering the
message he was supposed to deliver all along—I feel

the same stupid futility. Perhaps you know the story of Jonah, and how, at the end, Jonah finally tells the citizens of Nineveh that God's wrath awaits them, and how they repent, and how God ends up sparing their lives. This fills Jonah with anger. He's so angry he wants to die. Perhaps it's because he believes that the city's repentance is hollow, that God's mercy is undeserved. The last lines of the story are in God's voice. He asks Jonah how it could be right to condemn a city of a hundred and twenty thousand people who don't know any better—people who, as He puts it, don't know their right hand from their left.

Yours truly,
A concerned citizen

I started over, keeping it simple this time, leaving myself out of it as much as possible.

23

KING: I seen Antoinette. She said Damien got shot. You know what I'm saying? He got shot! He got shot! I was coming out the car and I seen her. He got shot, you know? That's why I had walked through the police tape. I wasn't thinking. I saw Antoinette and I just walked through it.

LAGARDE: Now, who is Antoinette?

KING: Antoinette. She live next door to Damien.

LAGARDE: Okay.

KING: She said he got shot. He got shot. She walking up the street and I said, "Y'all, you know, where y'all was at? Y'all didn't see nothing?" She say, "Oh, we ain't even ..." She said, "We ain't even ... We was inside the apartment." She said they was inside, in

the apartment next door, and all they heard was
cabinets slamming. I said, "What? What you mean?
Cabinets slamming?"

Lawrence stands at the door, sweat on his face, wearing slippers with high white socks, denim shorts over the gauze
wrapped around his leg where the bullet wound was. The
boys who were outside are gone now, their empty chair sitting on the asphalt beside a half-crushed can of iced tea.
Lawrence remembers stepping outside of Antoinette's
apartment into the glare and heat and seeing his car—a nothing car, a black Impreza—and thinking that he shouldn't do
this, but the mockery of the car cut deeper and deeper and
so now he's here.

"Just give me a minute," Damien says. He looks not just
tired but barely able to open his eyes in the brightness, the
apartment behind him completely dark from the blackout
curtains pulled up close against the windows. "What time
is it?"

"Let me get a Coke or something," Lawrence says.

"Come on. All right."

He lights a cigarette and backs slowly into the apartment and Lawrence follows him in, his eyes mucus-covered
slits. The living room is strung with lights like a bar, red and
white bulbs slowly blinking, the room receding, a brown
blur.

"You ain't hear nothing from Jodi?" Lawrence says.

"No."

"Not one phone call."

"I told you. I ain't heard nothing."

"I'm trying to tell you, I'm sick. I ain't feeling straight right now."

His throat goes tight, his eyes burning. It seems obvious from the party lights, the bellowing TV, that there's nothing here for him to find.

He walks upstairs and sees a rumpled comforter with green and red stripes, bundles of jackets and pants hanging from hooks screwed into the walls. He sees a picture on the dresser, Damien and his two girls, white ribbons in their hair, sitting on Damien's knees. He opens a dresser drawer and finds socks and underwear and three boxes of different types of cartridges but no gun, no money, nothing. He shuffles back downstairs, each step a wince of pain, the craving like a hunger for air now, a gasping in his veins.

"I need some help from you is what I'm saying."

"I told you, I ain't got nothing for you. I got maybe seven, eight dollars."

"Yeah. You said that. You keep saying that."

He points the gun just to the side of Damien's face. His own head is tilted, like someone patiently communicating with a fool.

"Don't do that, man," Damien says.

"Don't do that," Lawrence repeats.

24

We got up a little after five o'clock on Mardi Gras morning, very early, so that we could put on our costumes and visit some friends before the parade started. You have to live, even if you think you know better, I was telling myself. I was dressed as some sort of Hasidic zombie, with a black caftan, fur-trimmed cap, and a skull mask I'd brought back from Mexico City. Sarah was a lawn flamingo in a vaguely John Waters vein—she had a pink beak, pink wings, yellow tights, little squares of Astroturf with felt chicken feet glued to the tops of her shoes. We drank coffee, made Bloody Marys, then walked over to our friend Kevin's house, then to our friend T.R.'s house, then to the big gathering on Royal Street where the drumming had already begun. Kevin looked like a West African king this year. T.R. wore plastic pants and a gold lamé cape and space goggles and carried a huge black and gold umbrella. Deborah, whose outfit was so elaborate that I didn't recognize her at first, was the Star from the tarot deck, a moving cloud of cream

and pale blue tulle with a silver Venetian mask and silver
gloves. It was the first sunny Mardi Gras in a couple of
years, the sky full of reflected light from the river and the
white clouds constantly changing, as in the Caribbean, and
I had the vague feeling of walking through water as I entered the crowd, the colored streamers everywhere catch-
ing the mottled light—red, white, green, yellow, blue—all
the shotgun houses overrun by dragons, peacocks, sultans,
astronauts. When you wear a mask, you sometimes forget
that people can't recognize you, even people you know.
We were moving now, and it would be harder and harder
to cohere anyway. The plan was to follow this stream of
people into the French Quarter, then to try to make it to
Canal Street to catch the end of Zulu, the parade of the
historically black krewe whose members dress as outra-
geous stereotypes in grass skirts, with Buckwheat wigs and
giant fake cigars, and who bestow decorated coconuts upon
the crowd that throngs their floats. There was actually a
law in New Orleans that you couldn't sue for liability if
you were injured by a flying coconut on Mardi Gras day—a
fun fact I kept mentioning that morning. We were moving
along to the tinny beat of a karaoke machine on a decorated
wheeled cart playing disco. This would go on for several
hours, in the streets and in bars, at friends' houses and at
parties thrown by people we barely knew or didn't know at
all. There would be flasks of whiskey and bowls of gumbo,
plates of king cake and frito pie, fried chicken bought at
the gas station and plastic cups filled with wine, sangria,
gin and tonic. There would be a stop to see the Mardi Gras

Indians in their elaborate hand-sewn suits of ostrich feath-
ers and beads, the work of an entire year—the big chiefs
with their retinues of spy boys and flag boys, initiates in a
mystery cult and secret society of black pride. Maybe someone would catch a Zulu coconut. Maybe someone would
lose his fake cane, or lose his wallet. After a few hours, all
of this would agglomerate into a whirling ball of color and
sound and you might not care if you lost your wallet or your
fake cane in any case. We were in the middle of the French
Quarter now, the balconies jammed with tourists throwing
beads down on us, and Sarah was dancing in her flamingo
costume, stretching out her hands as wide as they could go,
then spinning, then prancing off, then spinning again. If it
doesn't sound graceful, then I'm not conveying it right. It
was the kind of grace that even the writer in the skull mask
was part of, brightly lit and grinning in the daytime crowd.

25

I started writing to Kendrick in the spring of 2015. Cathy
had left Angola for another job, and this meant that there
would be no more productions of the passion play, for the
play was her project, but it also meant that I no longer saw
any reason to honor my promise not to write to Kendrick
and others, not to engage in "pen pal" relationships. A long
time went by before Kendrick responded to my first note,
sent over JPay, the prison's e-mail system, for it turned out
he had been in lockdown, where he had no access to a com-
puter terminal. In lockdown, you're no longer in a dorm but
in a cage with a toilet and a sink and a bunk, either alone or
with a cellmate, and you're only allowed to leave the cage
for an hour each day. I never found out why Kendrick was
sent there. When he wrote back about three weeks later, he
greeted me in the name of his Lord and Savior Jesus Christ
and he went on in a similarly impersonal way. He said that
things were going well for him, that he was still in Bible college, working toward his ordination, and then he said that

he would never give up fighting for his release. The short
note somehow suggested that we were utter strangers and
always had been. It was a note of indifference, even of fare-
well. He said that he was going to think about filling out
the paperwork to apply for a reduced sentence based on his
good behavior, the first time he'd mentioned a new strategy
beyond the even more unlikely one of applying for asylum
in Saint Lucia. He closed by saying that one day I would understand that he had always been telling me the truth, but
the way he phrased it made it sound like he had long since
given up on that.

Baby steps, as he had once said about his own efforts to
educate himself. His note seemed to close off further com-
munication, so it took me a while before I responded. When
I started writing to him again, I learned that there were certain questions he wouldn't answer, and I learned that sometimes our correspondence was censored, that gaps would
appear, or the sequence of our e-mails would be broken,
and I could never tell in these cases if he wasn't answering my questions on purpose or because he simply hadn't
seen them. I asked him about the books he'd been reading
and I sent him the books I'd written, which he responded
to at length. In this way, we got to know each other better over the next few months. Some of the books he read
were familiar to me and others—self-help books, or books
about Egyptology or ancient Africa—less so. I asked him
about Theosophy, if he was still interested in that despite
his studies to become an ordained minister, and he said yes,
that he thought spirituality was "fluid." He said it was like a

house: you go into one room, he wrote, and see what light is there, then you go into another room and "maybe the light is brighter." He said that in Theosophy there's a figure called the Dweller on the Threshold who represents a person so bound by the past—not only his own past but the collective history of us all—that he becomes a specter, depleted, self-annihilating. In order to free himself, he needs to cross the Burning Ground, a trial not unlike what Jesus endured on the cross. We were talking again. I finally asked him about something he'd said the first week we met, something I struggled with for a while before I brought it up. That first week, he'd said that he knew who'd really done the murder with Lawrence but that he'd never say who it was because the person was only twenty years old then and didn't deserve to be where Kendrick was now. When I finally asked him about it, it was one of those questions he passed over in silence. I hadn't told him I'd seen Mason. I didn't have the courage to do that yet. But when he went silent, I had the troubling feeling that he somehow knew I had met Mason and that I had crossed a line. He sent me a brief e-mail after a few days that said he would write to me later, that something had happened and he thought he might be sent back to the cell block.

That was the last I heard from him for almost four months. There's a discipline board that meets every ninety days to consider which inmates should be taken out of lockdown and allowed to go back to the dorms, but if they rule against you, you have to wait another ninety days for the next hearing. The cell is painted white and has a small window, slightly smaller than a sheet of paper. The floor is gray cement. There's a stainless-steel vent that matches the stainless-steel frame of the bunk and the stainless steel of the toilet and sink. Sometimes you're issued an old-fashioned convict's jumpsuit, the kind with black and white stripes. Kendrick's silence, along with my ignorance of how long it would last, made me anxious in a way that is hard to describe. Inmates who have been in prison for a long time, leading lives of uncertain waiting, often find not only religion but esoterica such as astral projection or time travel in order to assuage their situation. My own version of this was my irrational feeling of responsibility, the sense that by asking Kendrick about who had really done the murder with Lawrence I had somehow caused him to get into trouble. I had brought back memories of Mason, whom I had to imagine was the person he thought he was protecting. *A clown type. A court jester type.* It was Mason whom he felt obliged to keep silent about, though Mason had abandoned him when he needed help and had never contacted him since, as far as I knew.

I never found out if this is what led to Kendrick being sent to lockdown for those nearly four months. When he finally got out, he wrote to say that he had been going to church the morning he got in trouble, that he had presented his ID, which he slipped through a slot in the glass for the guard to examine. The slot, he said, was just wide enough for the card, but the guard accused him of somehow throwing the ID at her in anger, though this would seem to have been physically impossible. This is what he told me, but there was always more that Kendrick couldn't or wouldn't tell me. We were speaking almost in code sometimes, overseen as we were by censors. After all this time, for example, he still hadn't told me if he'd ever written to the Innocence Project for their help. Every time I asked, he answered with silence. *There's a divinity that shapes our ends, rough-hew them how we will.* I found it easier to believe in the idea of fate during those nearly four months of silence, waiting for Kendrick to tell me what had happened to him. I knew that there'd been times in the last years that he'd wanted more from me, and now I was the one who wanted more from him, the one who checked his e-mail every morning, hoping for a message from someone who didn't respond.

I hadn't been back to Angola in more than a year. Whenever I did go back, I couldn't help but remember an incident that happened when I was covering the passion play with Deborah that first time. I was talking to an inmate named Joshua and as soon as we started talking, an assistant warden in a golf shirt and mirrored sunglasses and a corrections officer in a faded black uniform, gun at his waist, came to interrupt us. The warden put his face close to mine and yelled, "What are you doing here?" then he turned to Joshua and announced, "You're done," and just like that Joshua had disappeared. That day happened to be not just a rehearsal but an actual performance—there were spectators, people coming from the outside world, and so there was a security issue, and this assistant warden claimed that he didn't know

who I was. I tried to explain who I was. I told him that I'd
been there all week, doing a story with the photographer he
could see over there beneath the grandstand, that she and I
were with Cathy, and he yelled at me that no, I wasn't with
Cathy. "If you were with Cathy, you'd be with Cathy," he
said. I told him I had just been sitting with Cathy in the
grandstand—why didn't he call her with his cell phone and
ask? He walked away, leaving me with the guard, and I was
still so confused by this confrontation that it took me a moment to understand that I couldn't leave. The guard, who
could not have looked more like a guard, stepped closer and
asked me for ID. I gave him my driver's license and he examined it. My legs started to shake, absurdly. I told myself
to stop being ridiculous, that this wasn't serious, that it was a
misunderstanding that would be resolved soon, but my legs
went on shaking—reason didn't help. I made myself speak
up, telling the guard to call Cathy, and he told me that that's
what the warden was doing. At that point, the guard began
to ignore me and I became truly ridiculous. I was simply a
person standing there with nothing to do other than think
about the fact that I was standing there.

Another inmate I knew, Troy, approached, because he
was curious about what was going on, and I was struck by
how ashamed I felt to be seen by him like this. Troy knew
the guard and they started chatting. The guard took out
his phone and showed him some digital photos of a deer
he'd shot, and Troy pretended to be impressed. Then
they started gossiping about infractions, write-ups, and I
watched as Troy, who was opinionated and cynical, became

ingratiating, not out of weakness but out of tactics. We were both being humiliated, but Troy was in control of himself. I realized that one of the many differences between us was that my legs had just been shaking while Troy was calmly acting out a role.

The prison rodeo, which is open to the public, takes place every Sunday in October and one Sunday in April, and it was in April 2016 that I went there to try to see Kendrick among the crowd. I parked my car and walked through the muddy fields with my ticket, and when I passed through the gate I saw the concession stands—Fried Coke, catfish, pizza, jambalaya—and the INMATE RESTROOM, its walls decorated with that cartoon of the convict in prison stripes, the ball and chain around his ankle. It was hours before the rodeo was going to start but I wasn't there to see the rodeo. Kendrick said that he might be around in the multitude of booths set up for the inmate craft fair, an auxiliary event in which some of the men sell products they make in the prison hobby shop—salad bowls, wooden chairs, platters, even barbecue grills. They were out there in the open air or beneath huge metal overhangs in their street clothes, all but indistinguishable from the free people who were their prospective customers, though there was also a gallery of inmates around the perimeter behind chain-link fences who looked like prisoners from a Dickens novel—skinny, haggard, toothless, old and in wheelchairs, or young and grinning in self-loathing, many of them repeating the same joke:

you could always come back and buy from them later, they would say—they weren't going anywhere. The stalls and tables stretched on and on, several football fields' worth, huge tracts given over to hundreds of Adirondack chairs and rocking chairs and gliders and wooden coffee tables—more blond wood furniture than anyone could possibly buy, all of it skillfully made, some of it to an absurd degree. I asked around for Kendrick, and the inmates, some of them surrounded by their families, who had come to visit, tried to help me, their faces a blur of self-conscious neighborliness. It worked better when I gave them Kendrick's prison name, Dos, which made my face self-conscious in a similar way. There were paintings and toy ships and clocks and jewelry, lockboxes and perfect spheres of lathed wood that could be taken apart and put back together like puzzles if you learned the secrets of their workings. The drive from New Orleans had been three hours and I was hungry and thought about giving up and getting something to eat before I continued my search, but then I finally saw Kendrick, talking to another inmate beneath one of the metal overhangs in a quiet alley of tables and stalls in the shade. He wore jeans and a blue sweatshirt over a white T-shirt and he didn't have on his usual baseball cap. His hair was neatly cut, close to the scalp, and as his eyes met mine, his face looked a little fuller than before, the first sign that he had aged.

"I didn't know you made jewelry," I said.

He nodded, looking over at his display. "Something I picked up just recently."

We shook hands and gave each other a hug. I told him

that Sarah made jewelry and he seemed interested in this
and I looked at his work, mostly earrings which hung in
pairs from the wooden rack. I asked if he had heard any
news about Gary Tyler, who had been the director of the
passion play, the head of the inmate drama club, and who
was rumored to be about to be released, but Kendrick said
he hadn't heard anything beyond that. His earrings were
chased stainless steel, some just simple hoops, others in the
shape of zodiac signs or other emblems, intricately made,
perhaps from stencils. I told him that Sarah was a Leo, but I
didn't see any Leo earrings, so I kept looking for something
else as we talked. He asked me how she was doing and I told
him she was well and then I asked if he'd heard from Sonia
lately and he said yes, they had just talked a few days ago.
He told me that she still came to visit a few times a year, in
spite of her health. He said that she was on a list for a kidney
transplant, high enough up that she had gotten a phone call
a few months ago about a possible match, and it had made
her terrified that she was going to have to suddenly face the
surgery that very night, but then it hadn't worked out in
the end. They were both relieved, he said, though the relief
didn't really make sense, if you thought about it. I asked him
then if he'd heard from Aysha and he said no—he hadn't
heard from her in a while. No Aysha, no Marcus. Sonia—
that was his family for now.

"I think it's her mother," he said then. "Janelle, I think
she discourages her. But I'll see her. I'm not spending the
rest of my life in this place."

"I hear you."

He looked at me. "You don't understand. I'm not staying in here my whole life."

His eyes were fixed on mine but opened more widely
now and he seemed on the verge of saying something more.
He was close to tears of anger and the effort to restrain
himself made his whole body shake a little. He was standing close to me and not moving back, and I knew that the
anger was at me, that saying *I hear you* was insufficient, and
it was the first time I ever felt afraid of him. As all this
was happening, I saw out of the corner of my eye a group
of prison administrators heading toward us up the aisle we
were standing in. There were about eight of them, maybe
five assistant wardens and three guards, and I recognized a
number of their faces and even knew a few of their names.
I didn't want them to see me, so I looked down, hiding my
face. As they passed by, I saw myself through their eyes, a
sentimentalist who had formed a misguided attachment to a
violent felon he would never begin to know in any real sense.
But when I looked back up at Kendrick, I saw that he had
finally stopped shaking. Aysha had given up writing to him.
Sonia had almost had a kidney transplant. His nearly four
months in lockdown, I realized, had had nothing to do with
something upsetting I'd written to him in an e-mail.

"I'll get out," he said. "Believe that."

He said then that he'd heard that Antoinette was going
to write a letter saying that Kendrick had had nothing to do
with the murder. He'd heard this from a friend, he said, and
then he said that the next step would be to get Lawrence
to write a letter too. I told him that was good news and we

stood there in silence for a while. I knew how hard it was to
get out of prison, even if you were innocent. A lawyer friend
had described it for me once by drawing a set of nine boxes
on a napkin. Each column represented a successive avenue of
appeal: direct appeal, post-conviction relief, habeas corpus.
Each row represented the bureaucratic obstacles: district
court, state supreme court, federal supreme court. I knew
that Kendrick had already exhausted all nine of the boxes.
But I also knew how many prisoners had been exonerated
or released long after there seemed to be any hope.

We looked at the jewelry again. As so often in Angola, I
felt like some clueless Dante with no Virgil to be my guide.
There were no Leos, as I said, so I considered some other
designs—two fleurs-de-lis, a set of hearts, a set of crowns.
There was a pair of earrings whose shape I couldn't iden-
tify, and when I asked Kendrick what they were I couldn't
understand what he was saying at first. The shape was like a
heart with strange branch-like flames coming out at the top
on one side. It was a doe and a buck, he said. *A doe and a buck.*
I saw it then, the two ventricles of the heart also two deer
heads in profile, face to face, as if kissing. One of them, the
buck, had antlers that now looked nothing at all like flames.
The faces of the doe and the buck were idealized like car-
toons, but the heart, when you looked at it as a heart, was
jagged, as if ensnared in thorns.

"Those who see when they are shown," I said.

He didn't understand what I was referring to at first.

"Leonardo," I said.

"That's right, yeah, I remember that."

I realized that the reason I hadn't told him about seeing Mason was because I was haunted by the things I'd
imagined. What haunted me in particular was that my
imagining of Kendrick and Lawrence doing the murder together was at least as vivid as my imagining of Kendrick not
being there. In the first scenario, he was active, while in the
other he didn't do anything, and so perhaps it was no wonder that the first scenario, because it was more dramatic,
triggered my imagination. But perhaps it simply meant that
my imagination was more like Detective Lagarde's than I
wanted to admit. I didn't believe Kendrick had been there,
but I could envision it with clarity. My skill was to see
things in dramatic terms, but for this very reason it was
none of my business if Kendrick had or hadn't been there
on Athena Street. I couldn't get him out of prison. All I
could do was tell a story. *I talked to your cousin Mason and he
made me think you weren't involved.* That was all I had to say to
Kendrick now, but I couldn't say it. Because what if he had
been involved? Or, for that matter, what if he hadn't—what
if all these years he had been keeping silent about Mason,
and now, with Mason's part of the story revealed, there was
still nothing even a lawyer could do to get Kendrick free?
In that case, I would simply be reminding Kendrick of
something he already knew, which was that the story of his
innocence, amid many similar stories, had only a negligible
claim on the world's attention. He had implied this to me
the first time we met and I had not made much progress
since.

"I thought about him," he said, when I finally managed

to tell him about my visit to Meridian. "I thought about him for a long time. I thought maybe he was involved, that he was there. But you see the people in this place. I know these people. I know what people are like who have that in them. Mason, he ain't have that."

"You thought he was involved but then you changed your mind."

"I don't know what I thought anymore. It's been a long time."

"You must be angry at him for abandoning you."

"I'm not angry." He raised his chin, not looking at me, and shook his head a little, as if trying to remember some unimportant detail in a dream. "I just need to get out of here."

It was his facial expression that made me think that the uncertainty of the story would never end, only change. What he seemed to really be saying, I thought, was that he'd made peace with Mason, even though part of him still believed Mason had been involved in the murder, even though he would never say that, because Mason was his cousin and he loved him. He could never know for sure what had happened, and Mason could never tell him—I saw now that the guilt Mason had been carrying all these years was more complicated than I'd realized. It was the guilt of knowing that even if he'd come forward and told the truth from the very beginning—*I drove to Athena Street that morning, but I left before the murder happened*—it would have just sounded like he was lying. He probably would have gone to prison instead of Kendrick. That was the only choice Mason had ever had.

"That's good news about the letter from Antoinette," I said.

"Yeah. It's Lawrence I'm worried about. If he gets parole, maybe he'd write it. Otherwise, it's twelve more years before he gets out. I guess I could do twelve more years if I knew that would be it. Do that in my sleep."

"He'll write it."

He looked into the distance again, as if for confirmation.

He wanted to give me the earrings but I insisted on paying—they were five dollars. It was only when I got them home that evening that I noticed they had an un-expected connection to the tattoo Kendrick had on his arm, the one of the six-pointed star. I realized then that, like the six-pointed star, they were an emblem of the male principle in balance with the female principle, one side for each. Sun and moon, day and night, waking life and dream. *That's good news about the letter from Antoinette.* Astral projection, time travel, the letter from Antoinette, the letter from Lawrence ... There was a point, I realized, when my skepticism about Kendrick's hope became just an-other way of protecting myself from what was at stake. Like naïveté, the skepticism was just another kind of self-serving blindness.

26

In a theatrical flourish, the Lord and Savior Jesus Christ is resurrected as an inmate in the upper deck of the rodeo arena at Angola prison. He wears a white gown and a matching white headwrap, the fabric embossed with little circles of rhinestones, like a pattern of coins. The coins recall the thirty silver pieces that Judas, His betrayer, took as payment, but they've been transformed now, transfigured, made beautiful. Someone photographs Him from across the aisle and at the bottom of the stairs the *Angolite* reporter starts photographing Him too. There are a couple of women in the audience who have not stopped crying for the last hour and at the sight of this inmate in his white gown they cry even more, tissues in their hands, dabbing at their eyes as He raises His arms in His glory.

All the players in their biblical costumes are lined up in rows now, smiling, while the final theme music rises. Kendrick, Earl, Mary, Quntos, Taece, Layla, Gary, Wilbert, Cherie, Donald, Terrence, Pamela, Willie—there are more than seventy actors in the cast, too many to name. In unison they start singing, dancing, clapping on the twos and fours in celebration. It pulls them out of character, out of the ancient story and back into the present day, so that they just look like Americans, people from a certain time and place, some of them clumsier in their movements, some of them holding back a little, but all of them familiar with the ritual they're enacting, the inspirational swell of the closing anthem. There are big hornlike synthesizers, a repetitively triumphant chorus coming over the PA system. Jesus strides down the grandstand steps to rejoin His flock, His arms outstretched in benediction, and now the free people in the audience rise to their feet and start clapping on the twos and fours, for they know the ritual too. The cast of prisoners faces the free people, clapping, and the free people face them back, clapping, and it seems at first like a genuine image of offering and gratitude, of giving and receiving—the smiles on the actors' faces, the crowd smiling back—and in a certain sense it is genuine, but if you look to either side you'll see the grouped inmates also watching in the stands and you'll notice that they're not clapping, not smiling. Murder, kidnapping, rape, drug addiction, poverty, abuse, all pointing to the terminus—here. You can spend your life here for being present during a crime, even if you didn't commit it yourself. You can spend your life here for doing something stupid when you're sixteen. You can spend your life here for killing your girlfriend and setting her house on fire, or for killing someone like my father for money, or you can spend it here for doing nothing at all, an innocent person, or an exemplary one, like Kendrick, or like the protagonist of *The Life of Jesus Christ.*

Forgive us our trespasses, as we forgive those who trespass against us.

I've thought about that phrase many times and I'm still not sure whom it refers to or what it can possibly mean in this time and place.

I wrote another letter to the parole board. As of now, Kendrick has still not heard anything more from Antoinette.

On my desk, I have Deborah's photograph of him in his costume from the play. Aysha must have the same picture somewhere in the apartment in Houston. I remember that night I visited there and she came out of her mother's bedroom, having left her homework to eavesdrop on our conversation, and there was that brief moment when Janelle, before disciplining her, almost smiled at her, instinctively, seeing Aysha there in her school uniform. Recently, I interviewed a New Orleans street artist named Brandan "BMike" Odums, who told me that one of his work's themes is the ancient Greek distinction between chronological time— *chronos*—and a kind of ecstatic, heightened time called *kairos*, in which things happen eternally. Deborah's photograph of Kendrick, and that glimpse I caught of Janelle almost smiling at Aysha, seem like examples of what Brandan told me about, moments stolen from *chronos* and given to *kairos*, where there is no pain, because nothing ends.

PART FIVE

VISION

27

Why did ye take vengeance O ye sons of the mighty
    Albion?
Planting those Oaken Groves: Erecting these Dragon
    Temples…

—WILLIAM BLAKE,
"Jerusalem"

America I've given you all and now I'm nothing.

—ALLEN GINSBERG,
"America"

28

Janelle picked up the eyebrow pencil and with the index finger of her other hand pulled at the skin at the outer corner of her eye, looking straight into the mirror, trying to focus only on the eye and not on her face. The makeup felt dry going on, but the color slowly emerged in a line she carefully sketched in with slow, firm strokes. She didn't know how to put on makeup—her face was so plain that she didn't know if it even made any difference. Her eyes were bigger now. Her long lips were dark and red. A part of her could see that this was attractive, while another part of her looked on in disdain. Her face was a mask she moved behind, hair rising above her forehead, then falling straight down in braids behind her ears. The face was hers and it was not hers. It made her feel almost naked, walking across her bedroom behind that colored face.

Kendrick would look at her, not saying anything, and she would know that he saw something there that no one else saw, something they couldn't talk about, something she didn't even want to think about.

It was a quarter after ten. She walked quietly down the hall, eyes on the staircase, her coat gathered in a heap in one hand against her hip.

There was no one outside. She stood for a moment in the humid air, then put on her jacket and lit up a Marlboro from the pack she and Kendrick had bought the other night on Ursulines. She hugged herself in her coat, the moon bleeding through the thick cloud cover, and she thought of him backpedaling on the basketball court, his eyes locked on his opponent with absolute concentration, hand already extending as he closed the gap. It frightened her sometimes that he could lose himself in something so ordinary.

What light there was was a faint yellow, permeating the small room with a stillness. It cast subtle shadows over their bodies, bringing out the smaller curves, the mildest contours of her skin. In the half-light, he saw, they were the same faint shades of gray and bronze. The music on the radio broke in and out of the silence, a wash of static, then the distant, resonant echo of drums. The faintness of the shadows around her breasts made them seem more real. Her body in nothing but panties seemed more naked. He lay on top of her, his lips on the hollows of her shoulder, running his hand along her breast, feeling the folds of her nipple against his fingertips. Her lips were cool, the curve of the lower one almost rubbery between his own, but when she parted them the inside was warmer, moist with saliva. There was that glazed quality that things took on in bright sunlight when you had something caught in your eye. He could hardly see her in the gold light, feeling the warmth inside her panties, then bringing his face to her flat belly, resting it on her skin as he worked the elastic waistband over her thighs. The radio played only static now. He held her narrow waist between his hands, his thoughts confused, suffused now with the colors of the room, and she pulled him on top of her, eyes closed in the yellow light, pressing herself up into his grip. They lay on the narrow mattress and he could still feel her quivering inside him, her heartbeat thudding in his ear, faint and muffled at first, then louder, resounding, metronomic.

They were eighteen. That was how they had Aysha.

He's in lockdown again. He sits on the edge of the bunk with his eye swollen shut, his jeans a humid tent around his legs, no spot on his shirt that isn't damp from wiping his face. He takes his shoes off and stares at them, then he takes all his clothes off but his underwear and sits there on the cement floor with the bars at his side. He'll have to wash the clothes later in the toilet. He can hear a radio farther down the tier, a man screaming with no one there to scream at. He has a cut face and this tightness around his ribs even though he's quieted down, he's sitting quietly in the cell now, with a headache that makes him have to close both his eyes. Things are getting worse, not better. He'd made her some earrings in her zodiac sign, Virgo, the same as Janelle's. *Happy Birthday, Aysha, Love, Daddy.* It had been just two years ago on this day, her birthday, that she'd written him that first letter that got his hopes up.

29

LAGARDE: Okay. Is everything you've told me true and correct to the best of your knowledge?

KING: Yes, sir.

LAGARDE: Okay. And how do you feel you've been treated by me tonight, Kendrick?

KING: Fairly. Fair.

The back of the car is dark, the glass between him and Lagarde almost opaque, no air-conditioning coming in through the vent, the windows tinted so that everything outside is a field of bluish black with faint smudged pinpoints of white light. He sits like a child with his legs at an angle, his hands cuffed behind his back. There's a kind of cage built around the back of the car which adds to the feeling of absurdity, of overpreparedness, the cuffs on too tight, cutting

into the bones of his wrists and impeding the circulation in
his fingers. He sits without speaking in the dark blue space,
hearing the occasional noise of Lagarde's radio, with little
idea of where they are until Lagarde makes a turn off the
main road and he can somehow sense this is his mother's
street, Avenue F. He'd wondered as Lagarde had brought
him out after they'd made the tapes how he was going to get
his mother her car back—he had driven his mother's car to
the detective bureau. He had even asked Lagarde about it,
and Lagarde hadn't answered, just told him to stop straining. The blue-and-white lights are flashing but there's no
siren. Lagarde pulls into the empty driveway, the headlights
shining on the front of the house with such brightness that
you can almost hear it as a sound. He announces their ar-
rival on his radio, then reads out the number on the odom-
eter. Janelle and Desiree, Desiree and Janelle—after all that
back and forth, he has finally moved in with his mother, back
to this little house made of orange brick with a tiny cement
porch in front, two white columns, all of it lit up starkly
now like a scene from some crime show on TV. *Clean up her
face, Kendrick*. He remembers that moment at the Oakwood
mall, bent down over Aysha in the stroller to wipe her face
and seeing her cheeks, her nose, so intricate and small she
seemed to have been shaped from a mold, his baby girl, he
couldn't believe how it made him feel, Aysha, Janelle—his
girls. It's almost five in the morning but it's completely dark,
or at least it looks completely dark from inside the car. It's
the second time in a month he's been handcuffed in the
back of a police car. *Clean up her face, Kendrick*. Still looking

for a job, getting ready for school in a few weeks, thinking about becoming an EMT, all his clothes in garbage bags on the floor of his bedroom in his mother's house. He moves his fingers to try to get some blood into them, but the little movements make the cuffs bite into the bones of his wrist in a different, sharper way, his arms tingling now, pins and needles from the shoulders down.

They would examine his shoes and find there was no blood on them, they were almost as clean as if they were new. They would talk to Janelle and she would tell them he'd been home all day, then they would check the phone records and see she was telling the truth. He remembers her in the gold light, their bodies the same faint shades of gray and bronze, the music fading in and out into static. He can see his mother now standing outside the doorway in shorts and an oversized black T-shirt and he knows that she hasn't gone to bed tonight, that she's been waiting up for him all this time. She tries to move toward the car but all Lagarde has to do is make the slightest gesture, hardly raising his hand, to get her to stop. He has always felt a little superior to some of the people he knows because he has a mother from the islands, Saint Lucia, and he lived there once for a summer—lived also in New York, Chicago, Houston, Dallas—not just here. The last arrest he didn't even tell her about because it was so unconnected to who he was, so preposterous. He moves his fingers, his wrists inside the cuffs, and he tries to show his mother that he can see her but he can't tell if she can see him back. The brightness of the headlights, the flashing blue and white,

his mother and Lagarde starkly lit in the empty driveway—
all of it is real, but all of it looks like TV, feels like TV, some
distant scene he's watching through glass. It's real but it has
nothing to do with him. It isn't real. He still knows it will
all work out.

ACKNOWLEDGMENTS

Portions of this book appeared in a different form in the literary journal *Brick*.

I am grateful for an Award to Louisiana Artists and Scholars that gave me time and support while writing this book. I would also like to thank the following people: Jami Attenberg, Rob Bates, Roy Bridgewater, Bill Clegg, Donald Cousan, Earl Davis, Jennifer Davison, Taece Defillo, Willie Douglas, Jr., Cecilia Duncan, Joshua Ferris, Cathy Fontenot, Nicholas Gernon, Troy Grimes, Reginald Haynes, Mary Howell, Andy Hunter, Marshall Klimasewiski, Serey Kong, Rachel Kushner, Wilbert Marcelin, John McGhee, Le'Prease Montana, Cherie Perez, Michael Porché, Layla Roberts, Larry Sharp, Justin Singleton, Pat Strachan, Elton Thomas, Gary Tyler, Quntos Wilson, Tom Piazza, Lakesha Reed, Mark Singer, Billy Sothern, Levelle Tolliver, Bobby Wallace, Vernon Washington, Terrence Williams, all the people at Catapult, and most of all, my wife, Sarah.

Images from the series *Tooth for an Eye: A Chorography of Violence in Orleans Parish*, by Deborah Luster:

Part One
Ledger 01-02
Location: 1800 block of St. Roch
    (St. Roch)
Date: July 1, 2007
Name: Jeffrey Tate (65)

Part Two
Ledger 01-06
Location: Tulane Avenue at Dupre,
    Le Petit Motel (Mid City)
Date: April 4, 2008, 3:30 a.m.
Name: Unidentified Woman (20)
Notes: Gunshot wound to head

Part Three
Ledger 06-27
Location: 3000 block of Sandra Drive
    (Algiers)
Date: April 6, 2010
Name: Richard "Ricky" Temple, Jr. (30),
    Glenn's Cab Co. driver
Notes: Robbery. Gunshot to chest.

Part Four
Ledger 01-16
Location: 700 block of Burgundy Street
    (French Quarter)
Date: September 1978
Name: John M. Workman (34)
Notes: Stabbing

Part Five
Ledger 03-20
Location: Desire Street at North Claiborne
    Avenue
    (St. Claude)
Date: January 31, 2000
Name: Brian Moore (32)
Notes: Found face up in street